Multiverse
A novel

Robert Mercer-Nairne

GRITPOUL INC * WASHINGTON * USA

First edition 2020

ISBN: 978-0-9748141-8-6
Library of Congress Control Number: 2020901527

Published in the United States of America by Gritpoul, Inc.,
2025 First Avenue, Penthouse A
Seattle, WA 98121-3125
www.gritpoul.com

Interior Design and Typesetting: Danscot Ltd, Scotland
Cover Design: Larry Rostant, England
Front cover image: The Ancient of Days (etching with pen & ink, w/c and body colour on paper), Blake, William (1757-1827) / The Whitworth, The University of Manchester / Bridgeman Images
Author Photograph: Jill Furmanovsky - London

Printed by Friesens Corporation, Canada.

10 9 8 7 6 5 4 3 2 1

The paper used in this publication meets the minimum requirements of the American National Standard for Information Sciences – Permanence of paper for Printed Library Materials ANSI Z39.48-1948

In memory

Joseph E. Boyer

BY ROBERT MERCER-NAIRNE

POETRY

Mercer-Nairne in Malta

illustrated by Marisa Attard

On Fire

illustrated by Marisa Attard

PLAY

The Arrow

NOVELS

The Letter Writer

Like No Other

Warlord

The Storytellers

Multiverse

NON-FICTION

Notes On The Dynamics Of Man

A Paper (illustrated monograph)

The Damned and other essays

Multiverse - The Story

Set in the near future, the American economy has collapsed and depression era unemployment is rife. Banks are foreclosing on homes at an alarming rate sending families into makeshift camps which are appearing in the parks of all major cities.

Congress is paralyzed by gridlock between three parties each with a wholly different view about what needs to be done.

The still dominant Rationalists are holding to the position that the existing system which has brought prosperity to millions since the war, underpinned by scientific logic and free markets, is fundamentally sound and will self-correct.

Nationalists want to reverse globalization, rearm, and intern the dispossessed in 'Hospitality Centers' established in remote areas around the country – out of sight, out of mind.

Moralists argue that science and free markets have been allowed to function without any regard to their social purpose and that God must be put back at the center of the decision-making process.

Urged on by the charismatic evangelist Richard Preston, whose broadcast *God This Day* is widely followed, President Henry Dukes, a Moralist, is struggling to push his *Home Stabilization Initiative* through Congress.

Senator Milo M Meadows III, a Nationalist, wants to be the next president and is determined to thwart him. The Rationalists simply want to retain power and in order to do so will go with either the Moralists or Nationalists if they have to.

The backlash against scientific arrogance is preventing Carrie Holden, a budding astrophysicist, from getting her doctorate. Her childhood friend, Jay Chandler, is being encouraged to stand for the House as a Moralist by the San Francisco billionaire Marjory Anhauser, while President Dukes and Milo Meadows increasingly resort to the political black arts in their struggle for power.

The novel describes how these political tensions are resolved as well as how Carrie Holden and Jay Chandler's lives intersect. The title 'Multiverse' (drawn from *String Theory*, a strong contender for 'the theory of everything' beloved by physicists) speaks to the idea that many types of society are possible but that each is a child of its own moral tone or context and that during periods of disorder individual acts can determine long-lasting outcomes.

1

AS it had been for millennia past, the frontier was a draw for people like him: a place where a man could make his mark free from the moral constraints of social life subject only to the laws of nature. The excitement of discovery was primal, deep-seated within the human psyche. What lay over the next hill? What would unfold on the other side of the forest or around the next corner? The idea of virgin territory was libidinous. Once captured, its pull could make men mad, luring them on and on until requited, always a slender possibility, or left to flounder in an unforgiving wasteland where the only solace was perpetual hope in the face of hopes dashed like screes of broken rock.

To be able to return to the very world one had abandoned

and say 'I have found something of great value; I ......' and to be applauded, fêted, talked about, admired and written into history; that was the purest gold, the greatest gift, the ultimate reward. What mattered was not what was found because what was found was already there, but that its existence became known to those with whom one identified, opening up possibilities for them that they had not previously entertained. Possession and exploitation: the passionate devouring out of which new life mysteriously came, unplanned and driven, solitary and yet dependent. Nature thrived on such frontiers and physics was John Franks's.

It had only been ten years since his lecture had gone viral. With hindsight, the timing could not have been worse. The recession which had been gathering force at the time had now turned into a depression and fear was everywhere. For him, 2013 had been a very good year. The Nobel Prize followed by the Newton Chair at the prestigious Center for Advanced Physics. He'd had his eye on CAP for several years and beaten his colleague Reyansh Singh to the post. Reyansh still hadn't forgiven him. They'd worked together but he had published first. It had doubtless helped that he was already a star on the lecture circuit. Reyansh's plodding style could empty a lecture hall in moments, if word hadn't already got out so that it started that way. The academic world took no prisoners. That was the way of it. He clicked on the YouTube link to enjoy himself once more.

As he gazed at his doppelgänger telling the audience in the darkened auditorium about the simple majesty of String Theory while clever visuals burst behind him like stardust illustrating things alien to the everyday mind, he wondered if the conjecture which had gained him his prize would prove to be true. He strongly believed that it would. The theory's sheer beauty was

CHAPTER 1

compelling: tiny filaments of primal energy vibrating at just the right pitch to sustain the exact relationships that underpinned our universe. Another pitch, another set of relationships – another universe. Ours was one amongst many in a multiverse bound together through quantum entanglement.

Ah the applause! He played the ovation back again. There was no better drug and he'd tried most.

His lecture still hadn't been taken down. He knew it would be eventually. It was only a matter of time.

Just then Carrie Holden, one of his PhD students, put her head round the door.

"John, you'd better hurry up. The Dean wants to start."

Carrie had so far refused his advances, in spite of the effect it might have on her prospects. She was bright and with something of a conscience, which reminded him of his own buried deep beneath departmental rivalry and an undisguised drive for acclaim.

* * *

Dean Jimbalaya looked distracted, not his normal suave, assured self, the epitome of the successful fund-raiser and administrator he had become when his career as a physicist had rolled into the rough.

"Is everyone here?" he asked, looking distractedly toward his secretary who was the only one in the room other than him

CHAPTER 1

to know the nature of what was about to be imparted to his audience.

"Yes Dean, I believe so," she answered, checking once more the neat ticks she had appended to the names on her list.

As befitted, by their own estimation, some of the smartest free-thinkers on the planet, mostly male, those assembled slumped in chairs around the room in no discernible order betraying mild irritation that they had been removed from their incessant calculating for which they were handsomely paid by a society that had only a tenuous grasp of what they actually did.

Dean Jimbalaya cleared his throat in an unsuccessful attempt to gain attention. His secretary, who was well practiced in getting the Center's highly charged egos to do as they were told, announced in a firm, clear voice "The Dean!"

The chatter subsided and all eyes arrested on a principal who played a remarkably small part in their lives save when it came to hiring them. No one could recall when one of their body had been fired. Even gross misconduct of a personal nature was rapidly brushed aside in the interest of science.

"I am afraid I have some disturbing news," he began.

The political situation in the country, indeed around the globe, was poor; they knew that of course but they were hardly likely to be affected. They were humanity's problem solvers after all. 'Disturbing news' had no greater ring to it than would the death of a past practitioner of their craft whose ideas had long since been superseded. A few wondered whose funeral they

CHAPTER 1

would be attending so as to ensure a reasonable showing at their own and whether it was cause that would link the two events or merely correlation.

"There is no easy way to put this," Dean Jimbalaya declared, "but CAP is being closed down."

It might never have happened before. Six top class physicists were lost for words. It was as if the Dean's announcement had been sucked into a Black Hole from which nothing but radiated disbelief could escape.

Although unnerved by the silence he limped on.

"Well not closed down entirely," he modified, "absorbed within the Marjory Anhauser Theological Institute."

The wife of Bill Anhauser, the great internet tycoon now deceased, Marjory had endowed MATI, as she asked that it be called, with a billion dollars, one of the largest single donations ever made. The task of her institute was to rebuild religion in America.

"For fuck's sake!"

The words of the thirty-year-old particle physicist, Josh Rodriguez, himself in line for a Nobel Prize, sounded like a rifle shot on a still day and everyone sat in silence wondering who had been hit.

"Well, I'm emigrating," growled Doug MacLachlan whose work on quantum field theory was still much admired.

"I am afraid that won't be possible," cautioned Dean Jimbalaya. "By executive order President Dukes has banned all physicists from leaving the country."

"Oh, for fuck's sake!"

Josh Rodriguez was more adept with differential calculus than he was with words. That said, he had accurately encapsulated the sentiment that pervaded the room which now buzzed like a disturbed hive.

"What about our pensions?" asked Naomi Sanchez whose work on quantum fluctuations had earned her the grudging respect of her male colleagues.

The Dean, who had started drawn and white turned whiter still.

"The President has confiscated these by executive order," he answered.

"He can't do that!" protested Gary Wipfler.

"I am afraid he just has," Dean Jimbalaya corrected. "And I have to tell you, the mood in the country is sour, really sour. Perhaps I have shielded you for too long. It can hardly have escaped your notice that a growing number of people out there hold the ideas of physicists in utter contempt."

Of course it hadn't. But weren't there always stupid people in the world? No one said as much, but that is what they felt.

CHAPTER 1

One of the janitors rushed into this febrile atmosphere and was barely noticed, until his anxious words defined a new reality.

"There's a crowd approaching our building," he gasped, "and it looks real angry."

CHAPTER 1

CHAPTER 1

2

THE race for the exit – any exit leading away from the mob – had been unseemly. Dean Jimbalaya's somewhat plaintive "good luck colleagues" had done little to calm nerves. Everyone knew about the attack on the research facility outside Detroit the previous week but never imagined such a thing in New Jersey.

In a reversal of roles John attached himself to his PhD student like an eager puppy. His car was out front. He hoped hers would be in the student lot way down the hill at the back.

"You did drive in?" he shouted out as they hurtled down the back stairs.

"You want a ride?" she called back.

"I wouldn't mind," he answered with unconvincing casualness.

She looked spectacularly attractive in flight, he thought.

"Why don't you come up?" he proposed when they reached his apartment block. He'd read that drama could act as a powerful aphrodisiac.

"Not right now," she told him, wishing to keep the possibility of a relationship based on something other than differential equations alive for a little longer. "I have a big drive ahead of me."

"To your parents?"

"Yes."

"That is a drive. How long will it take?"

"Five days."

Five days in a car. He couldn't imagine why anyone would want to put themselves through that.

"Why don't you fly?"

"It gives me time to think. Besides, a six-thousand-mile round-trip puts the space-time continuum into perspective."

CHAPTER 2

He took her remark seriously, which she had not intended, and wondered what he might be missing. In his line of work thirty-five was getting old and twenty-three-year-olds like Carrie were an ever-present threat.

"Jees, do you hear those sirens?" With his concentration now released from what had become a diminishing possibility, the outside world burst in. "It must be wild back there."

They both listened to the wailings and whinings of police cars, fire trucks and ambulances, each vying for attention.

"Well, I'm out of here," Carrie announced. "I only came in to hear Dean Jimbalaya tell us we were doomed. I was already packed and ready to go. Hope your car's OK."

The Nobel laureate looked on as she drove off and wondered why life was harder to manipulate than his calculations, although even they did not always do what he wanted.

* * *

Carrie headed south out of Princeton and then swung west above Philadelphia passing Fort Washington, Lafayette Hill and Plymouth Meeting, all names that meant something in the history of her still young country, before joining Interstate 78 by Valley Forge where General Washington had held his army together as the British swaggered around Philadelphia. Her mother wondered why she hadn't gone to Stanford, but Carrie knew the West Coast and wanted to experience the East with all its history. She devoured history but had been unusually good at math which had drawn her toward physics, although cosmology was her chief interest. She'd already been offered a job at one of the Mauna Kea research facilities on Hawaii where the height and absence of light pollution made it easier for people like her to gaze up into the heavens. She knew this irritated John who preferred his students to be dependent, although she still needed him to sign off on her doctorate.

The state of her poor country concerned her greatly. Economic life had never fully recovered from the financial collapse of 2008. No one quite knew why. There were plenty of ideas. Things had looked as though they were healing but then world trade fell off a cliff. Globalization had been blamed for a lot of ills and its consequences had probably not been handled very well. And then there was automation. Whole communities had found that their skills were no longer needed. The work that had given them decent lives had either been exported to developing countries where wages were low and populations were growing, or had been taken over by smart machines. A new breed of politician had come to power on the back of this, railing against foreigners, immigrants and science. Barriers had been erected and trade had collapsed. And now climate change was causing crop failures across the Midwest.

People were dispirited and science was often being blamed. John Franks's lecture, at first something of a sensation – although not so much among physicists and cosmologists as the general public – heralding the possibility of the multiverse, had since become toxic. *Humanity the great irrelevance* read one headline, *So alone – what's the point?* read another. Increasingly progress and what was branded as arrogant knowledge were being seen as the villains that had brought people to the state they were in. Most of her academic colleagues had been happy to ignore these

CHAPTER 2

protests as the mouthings of the ignorant, but for how much longer?

She pulled into a motel on the outskirts of Toledo, exhausted.

* * *

The following day Carrie made it to Iowa City, a seven hour drive. She had left behind what remained of America's industrial heartland, the product of an earlier age. Pittsburg, Detroit, Chicago – each had had its moment, its own Big Bang, and each had had to reinvent itself when that moment faded: Carnegie's steel empire in Pittsburg, Ford's automotive one in Detroit, and Chicago as the point from which manufactured goods fueled America's westward expansion while cattle and grain from her pioneering frontier were being shipped back to feed the teeming masses spilling into her eastern cities from Europe. Chicago seemed to have done best, producing Al Capone, the Teamsters Union, Mayor Richard J. Daley and Barack Obama: a tough city that had worked.

But it wasn't until she stopped on the third day at a diner on Interstate 80 just shy of Malcolm – population 290 she read, 98% of them the descendents of white Europeans – that she was freed from her own thoughts. The place wasn't busy and a couple in their sixties, no doubt spotting new blood, decided to engage her in conversation.

"Traveling far?"

She'd been brought up in a small town where people talked

and strangers were interesting, so the man's question did not surprise her.

"California."

There was no rush to respond and the waitress came over to 'freshen them all up' with a refill of watery coffee. Starbucks had been kept at bay.

"You OK traveling alone?"

The woman's question mixed concern, interest and mild disapproval in equal measure.

"Yes."

"A storm's coming," the woman told her, "so you'll need to be careful."

"You're used to storms here, I guess. My parents moved west from these parts and told me all about them."

"Is that right?" the man interjected, warming to the possibility of a connection. "They'll be a whole lot worse now I think. Folk round here are lucky if they get one good crop in three. Soon it'll be one in four and that will be the end for most of them."

John Steinbeck's *Grapes of Wrath* came to mind. Farmers fleeing the Midwest dust bowl for a better life in California and being blocked by vigilantes and police at the state border. She'd loved that book. Steinbeck had come from the Salinas

CHAPTER 2

Valley next to her home town. Like her, he'd moved east. East-West; Americans always seemed to be on the move in search of something better.

"Can I ask what you do, dear?" the woman asked.

"I am training to be a scientist," Carrie told her. "Physics, mathematics, cosmology – I haven't quite decided. Although each likes to be different, they all play off one another. I think it will be cosmology."

"Is that right?" The note of disapproval had crept back into the woman's voice.

"I don't much hold by that theory of everything," the man said. "If we really knew everything we would not be in such a mess."

"Science has done a lot of good things," Carrie asserted.

"And a lot of bad things too," the man answered back. "Do you know how many churches there are right here?"

"I am afraid I don't," Carrie readily admitted, wondering how they had moved onto this new ground.

"Well there's the United Methodist, the First United Presbyterian and Trinity Lutheran," he told her, "and that's just here in Malcolm. Can you imagine how offensive it is to people when they are told that scientists have unlocked the secret of the universe?"

CHAPTER 2

"My husband minds about that," the woman apologized, not wishing to offend a stranger she looked upon as their guest. "Where's your next stop?"

"I hope to make North Platte by nightfall."

"Well you take care now," the woman urged as she and her husband got up to leave, "and be mindful of that storm."

As Carrie watched them go the man turned and said that her parents had been right to leave. She felt a strange attachment. America had grown out of people like that and to be part of something that caused them hurt concerned her.

The waitress who had been watching – there was little else to do – sashayed over.

"Freshen up hon?"

"No, I don't want to have to make any unscheduled stops.

"It goes right through you, don't it."

"A nice couple," Carrie said, almost to herself.

"Yes, that was Esther and Frank Pierce. Good folk. They eke out a living five miles north of Malcolm, but its hard right now, real hard."

She drove off and as foretold, was soon enveloped by a storm of biblical proportions, with rain the wipers could barely clear and wind gusts that threatened to lift her car aloft like

CHAPTER 2

Dorothy's home in Kansas. Carrie wondered if she would ever find a partner like Frank Pierce and whether he and she would ever be thought of as 'good folk'.

As the miles passed a much bigger thought fought its way to the surface. What had really happened back there in New Jersey? Her university had not been closed down, just the Centre for Advanced Physics. It was government funded so she guessed the government could do what it liked. Truth be told, she had quite enjoyed watching a room full of prima donnas lost for words. But CAP had been deliberately targeted: that was worrying.

The political atmosphere had certainly been poisonous for several years and was getting worse as the lives of more people spiraled out of control. Henry Dukes had been elected president promising to call to account all those who he said were destroying America's true values. 'Ours is one nation under God' he'd said, a mantra repeated countless times during his successful campaign.

Liberalism and the permissive society seemed to have run their course and value neutral science was now regarded by many as the vessel from which evils were being unleashed into the world like the one uncorked by the curious Pandora of ancient Greek legend. Carrie knew her kind was privileged. Had the university not agreed to cover most of her costs and pay her for the undergraduate teaching she did, she would not have been part of it.

As others struggled to make ends meet the value of the academic aristocracy was being called into question. Frank Pierce was not the only person to have an almost visceral dislike of any claim that the universe could be reduced to a few numbers,

CHAPTER 2

however fancifully arranged. President Dukes appeared to be using the force of this anger to help him dig the nation out of the hole it was in. This did not bode well. She'd read enough history to know what followed when hatred was unleashed.

CHAPTER 2

3

HENRY Dukes liked biographies and considered himself a straightforward man who spoke plain. He had been married to the same woman for forty years and went to church on Sunday. The popular rhetoric and verbal incontinence of his predecessor were alien to him. As the governor of Wyoming he had run a tight ship and although one of the least populous states in the Union, saw no reason why his presidential administration should run along different lines. Knowing that he was regarded by the East Coast establishment as an unsophisticated mountain boy, in spite of being sixty-three and having reached the rank of major general in one of his country's interminable wars, he had appointed Seymour "SS" Stone as his Attorney General. A diminutive man with thick glasses, sparse hair and a high voice who had a nose for human weakness, Stone knew not only the corridors but the back passages of power and was widely feared.

The President moved the papers on his desk a little to the left and then moved them back again a little to the right. There weren't many and they were well ordered. He did not like a cluttered desk.

He'd been in the oval office before of course but as the governor of a state with only one seat in the House of Representatives and three electoral votes his views had carried little weight. Even the high-flown annual economic policy symposium at Jackson Hole functioned largely without him. How things had changed. People were searching for certainty and his simple homespun message had secured him his party's nomination and then the presidency. As he saw it, America was hungry for God and with the parable of the five loaves and two fishes as his guide, he would deliver. The intercom on his desk clicked open.

"Attorney General Stone is here to see you, Mr. President."

"Have him come in Eunice."

He'd brought his secretary with him from Cheyenne.

"Yes Mr. President," she acknowledged. "Now unless there's anything else, I'll be going."

"No dear, that's it for the day. I'll see you Monday. Have a good one."

"You too Mr. President."

CHAPTER 3

He knew Eunice was missing the mountains. How could one not? He would like to have gone after a trout or two himself. But there was a job to be done and she was as committed as he.

"SS, come on in."

"Mr. President."

Stone's high falsetto voice had a mesmorising quality to it that drew you in like a Latin mass. Whether what he was saying was good or evil seemed less important than how he was saying it. As a Methodist, Henry thought there was something Catholic about Stone, but didn't hold that against him. Apostasy was blind to denomination. They sat down opposite one another on the comfy sofas and a staffer brought in a tray with two glasses and a jug of lemonade. As far as he knew, his guest had never touched alcohol, another characteristic that distanced him from most of the Washington crowd.

"Where are we with the religious leaders SS?" he asked. They had drawn together the names of all the most prominent preachers, those with the longest reach, to see if some sense of political direction could be established.

"They are keen to be led out of the wilderness Mr. President, but their traditions are separate and of course the Constitution guarantees them freedom from government."

"Quite so," the President acknowledged, "but it is not religious approach we are interested in. It is the struggle between belief and doubt. The hardships people are experiencing are causing them to lose faith in a social order that was not religious but supposed to be managed and scientific. We cannot ask them to have faith in what has failed. We have to rebuild faith around something new."

"Faith on its own won't feed families Mr. President."

"I understand that, damn it. But I can't short-circuit our failed systems without cover. The truth is we lost our way. We became too self-centered, too greedy, and we thought science had all the answers when we weren't even asking the right questions. Values matter. You know that. I know that and probably everyone else knows that. But by placing value-free science on the altar of our secular church we forgot and started to act as if values did not count. We are now paying the price, not because our systems were intrinsically bad but because we used them unwisely. Only with God back at the center of our lives, however we choose to address that great receptacle of eternal values, will we recover our sense of balance."

Seymour Stone allowed himself a thin smile.

"I have never heard God described as a container before Mr. President!"

At first Henry looked perplexed. He knew words could be a tangle.

"If I say 'Him' I'm in trouble; if I say 'Her' I'm in trouble; if I say 'It' I'm in trouble. At least receptacle keeps me out the clutches of the LGBTQ people, or however many letters we've got to. You can see why religious discourse is so difficult. Mind you, it is no more contrived than quarks, gluons or the Big Bang.

CHAPTER 3

Anyway, the point is that God, as a single shared expression of what we are, needs to be put back at the center of people's lives – period: a complete change of culture."

"We've made a start Mr. President."

"Detroit and New Jersey: I read about that – violence to channel violence."

"It's best you keep your distance."

"How much more do we need?"

"As much as it takes to put science, especially the science of creation, back into its box." The Attorney General's words had a lyrical clarity about them as he went on: "horror and hate are fundamental to human nature. They are our teachers. Horror tells us what we should fear; hate tells us what we should destroy. We have to make examples of what must be hated, in a manner that invokes fear."

President Dukes lent forward to reach the jug and filled his and the Attorney's glasses.

"Scientific privilege should be hurt, particularly the arrogant sort", the President stressed, "the kind that treats mankind as some sort of mathematical residual - as a goddamn nonentity. If horror and fear will help me bind this country back together again, then I need horror and I need fear. Right now things are falling apart. People have lost faith in authority. And when authority lets so many down, I can't blame them. There is real hatred out there SS. We need to control that hatred before it controls us."

Attorney Stone sipped his lemon as if he was savoring a fine wine.

"The preachers must pull their weight," he said in his sing-song voice. "There has to be a new vision of hope."

The two men talked about trivia for a while, although in this SS was clearly out of his depth. The retired general tried to interest him in the subject of fishing, but without success. The flow of conversation improved briefly when Henry recalled the awkward court-martial case that had brought them together, but neither man had much appetite for it. Thanks to Stone the army had been protected but an innocent soldier sacrificed: another casualty of war. When the Attorney General took one last sip of lemonade and made his excuses it was a relief for them both. He left, passing the President's wife in the corridor on her way in.

"I don't know why you appointed that man, Henry," she said when the President's departing guest was well out of earshot. "He's really not very nice."

"Power has its dark side, Mary. Always has had and always will."

She shrugged her shoulders dismissively.

"Try not to be late dear," she counseled. "The Reverend Preston and his wife Abigail are joining us for dinner. We'll be in the private quarters."

CHAPTER 3

4

"Dr. Preston, welcome to the White House. This is a rare pleasure!"

President Dukes was excited. The Reverend Richard Preston had become a legend who he longed to meet. At over six foot two with a fine angular face and brindle hair, his youthful features and physical intensity were impossible to ignore. The pastor filled his church in Annapolis to bursting and was listened to by millions across the nation on his internet link *God this day*.

"Mr. President, Mrs. Dukes," their guest acknowledged shaking their hands and presenting his helpmate, "my wife Abigail." The pastor's wife, a petite, attractive woman with raven black hair and a strong face, stepped forward to greet the presidential couple. "Let me assure you both," Richard Preston insisted, "the pleasure is ours."

The family dining room had an air of intimacy, but was still smart with rich red velvet curtains, yellow silk on the walls and a white carpet with blue swirls, chosen by Mrs. Dukes. Hanging above the sideboard opposite a marble fireplace and the gilt-framed mirror above it was Henry Ossawa Tanner's *Annunciation*, on loan from the Philadelphia Museum of Art, depicting a woman in the presence of God's messenger.

When they were seated the President invited his guest to say grace.

Richard Preston lent forward slightly, his hands clasped under his chin and his eyes fixed on the center of the table in deepest concentration.

"Almighty God," he began, "bless this house, these people and this government and let us give thanks for what we are about to eat, knowing that there are a growing number in our great American family who are without. Through Your grace, help us to find a way out of this darkening nightmare and the will to lead our people to a better place. Amen."

The President's "well said" felt small and inappropriate and he wished he hadn't said it.

"How was your drive here?" Mary Dukes enquired turning to Abigail.

CHAPTER 4

"Just under an hour," she answered. "We encountered no disturbances. But the encampment in front of the White House is upsetting."

"It grows every day," the President told her. "I guess folk want to be near their government, near to me even, in the hope that we will do something."

"Soup kitchens have been set up," Mary explained, "so people are being fed. But winter is approaching and it can only get worse. It's the children I worry about. We are trying to get a temporary school established."

"Mary's been tireless," Henry affirmed. "She does things that matter. I sometimes feel that we politicians are just spinning our wheels."

"I have a suggestion, Mr. President," Richard Preston announced, "if you will allow me."

"Goddamn it pastor, I surely need suggestions," the President responded, trying to ignore his wife's look of disapproval at his turn of phrase, a look that made Abigail smile. "If you've got an idea, now is the time and here is the place."

"The Food Stamp program is working. You have extended it indefinitely, or at least until this crisis is behind us. That's good," he said. "But the government must go further. People are losing their homes at an alarming rate. Women and children are ending up in sports halls, and many of the young men are running loose. As you would expect, criminality is on the rise.

CHAPTER 4

"Just this week a mob entered our exclusive Epping Forest neighborhood and ran riot. The residents were terrified. The community police were called and two men were shot, but the rest ran off. There were no arrests. There are just too many footloose citizens for our police to cope. By the time the National Guard is called out the disturbance has moved elsewhere."

"Yes, I'm getting similar reports from across the country," the President confirmed. "So what is your proposal pastor?"

"A home voucher scheme. The downward spiral must be stopped. People have to be kept in their homes."

"Are you suggesting that the government underwrite the unemployed's rent and mortgage payments?"

"Yes I am."

Henry Dukes let out a whistle as his mind grasped the enormity of the idea.

"I'd never get that through Congress," he murmured, mostly to himself.

"Well I think that's an excellent idea," Mary Dukes extolled. "People get to stay in their homes; banks and landlords are made whole; money is fed into the economy. It might just get us moving in the right direction again."

"But the cost Mary, the cost," Henry muttered. "It would be frightening."

CHAPTER 4

"Isn't where we are right now frightening, Mr. President," interposed Abigail, in support of the sisterhood and her husband.

"Administering such a program would be dreadful," the President calculated, still trying to grasp the full measure of what had been suggested. "This is public money we are talking about. Can you imagine the bureaucrat at the counter working out what claim was genuine and what claim was not? There would have to be rules and the whole thing would get bogged down before it had begun."

"Well, I have a proposal there too, Mr. President," Richard Preston advanced.

"Oh, alright let's hear it," the President wearily invited.

"I propose that the entire home voucher scheme be administered through the churches."

Henry Dukes sat in silence. One novel idea before bedtime was bad enough, but two: that invited extreme indigestion. Even Mary was speechless. It took Abigail to puncture the sound of pins dropping in the family dining room.

"Rules, Mr. President, can only ever take us so far. Commitment to the right path comes from belief. If the churches were to administer the home voucher scheme" – in Abigail's mind it had already moved beyond an idea to an actuality – "the church community would know full well who was genuine and who was not."

CHAPTER 4

"I can see a rapid uptick in church attendance," ventured the President.

"That's as may be," continued Abigail. "But if we want to rebuild communities, isn't that exactly what we need?"

"I tell you, there will be more joy in heaven over one sinner who repents than over ninety-nine righteous persons who need no repentance – Luke 15 verse 7." The pastor's words were delivered with a quiet force that arrested even the White House butler as he gathered up the plates from the first course.

Noticing this, the President turned to him.

"Well, what is your view, Matthew?"

"Between a tent on the White House lawn and my own home, Mr. President, I know which I'd prefer."

"So there you are, Henry," applauded Mary. "All you have to do is make it happen!"

"I'll have to run this one by Senator Grasser," ruminated Henry who was beginning to see some advantage in the idea. "If anyone could drive it though the senate, he could. The lower house is a different matter. Those boys and girls are running around like squawking fowl crying 'the sky is falling, the sky is falling' and I can't get an iota of sense out of them. Someone needs to send a fox into that coop."

"Then their sky <u>would</u> start falling," remarked Mary.

CHAPTER 4

"And they probably wouldn't realize until too late," countered the President acidly. "They need to be frightened into right action and rewarded for taking it: heaven and hell. That's where you come in, pastor."

"When it comes to Heaven and Hell I've always been more New Testament than Old, Mr. President: carrots over sticks."

"We're surely creating hell enough right here on Earth," observed Mary, "without emphasizing another one. What we need is a way out."

"Which is why bolstering the role of the churches makes sense," urged Abigail. "People will come to see that faith in moral behavior is more important than economic advantage or disadvantage."

President Dukes made a 'note to self' that Hell was clearly his domain.

"So pastor," he said, "do you think you could persuade the other churches to cooperate on such a scheme, if I could get Congress to approve it?"

Richard Preston might have been a man of God but he also had an acute understanding of Man.

"It would have to be kept to the traditional denominations," he answered. "Otherwise we'd have sects springing up everywhere. Factionalism has been religion's curse."

"You are surely not suggesting that the Reformation was a

CHAPTER 4

mistake now pastor, are you?" the President asked with just a hint of mischievousness.

"I'll pass on that."

"A most diplomatic answer!" the President conceded.

"What about those people who are not affiliated with any religion or denomination?" Mary asked.

"They'll just have to pick one," Abigail interposed. "Our purpose here is to rebuild God-centered, moral communities. Form is not the issue."

"And those who don't believe in God?" Mary wondered.

"Let's leave them to the physicists," the President chuckled.

"There will always be difficult issues, Mr. President," Richard Preston conceded, "but I can tell you this. Our church will not turn away anyone in need. The parable of the Samaritan is at the heart of everything we do."

Later that night, after his guests had set off on their return journey to Annapolis and his wife was preparing herself for bed, President Dukes called Arlen Grasser.

CHAPTER 4

5

CARRIE came down from the north into Gilroy on Highway 101. For most of its life her home town had been a small sleepy place except when the Mexican pickers arrived to harvest the crops growing in the Salinas Valley to the south. Since the 1950s the city's population had increased tenfold, but these days signs of distress were everywhere. What had once been gleaming new subdivisions were peppered with weather-worn *For Sale* signs and there was not a Mexican picker in sight. The Nacimiento and San Antonio reservoirs had all but dried up, the water table had disappeared and the Salinas River was now a ribbon of sand all year long. What had once been dubbed America's salad bowl was fast becoming one of its deserts.

When her family moved west her father had secured a job as the manager of the Castro Valley Ranch, a magical property in the hills above Gilroy owned by the Chandlers, a wealthy family from San Francisco. A simple white-painted wooden house next to the yard where the ranch equipment was stored and about a mile from the ranch house itself came with the job. Old man Chandler did not operate the ranch for profit but for pleasure and conservation. His grandson Jay, three years older than Carrie, had been her first love. "Now don't you go gettin' involved with that young man," her mother had warned. "Your father doesn't need the complication." But nature wasn't listening and old man Chandler seemed to like her and no harm had come of it. Then college appeared over the horizon, as it does at that age, and they had drifted apart.

She ascended the narrow winding road from the town, hoping not to meet anyone driving down. Eventually the car made it to the ridge and her spirits rose. A short flat section still lay ahead before the way turned down and the Castro Valley opened out in front of her like Shangri La. The ranch lay inside a fold in the hills running south-east to north-west, rising gently to a higher ridge at the top end from which one could look down toward Monterey Bay and the Pacific Ocean. The sea mist brought moisture to the crest sustaining the most southerly stand of giant redwoods before drought-tolerant live oaks took over. She and Jay had discovered each other on that ridge.

As Carrie approached the steading she could see her mother beating a rug draped over the picket fence. Dust was Madge Holden's enemy, cleaning was her solemn duty and water was her essential ally. Unlike the valley below, the ranch was not short of it and their well had always been forthcoming.

CHAPTER 5

None-the-less, the Chandlers had built a reservoir in the trees near the ranch house and 'the Holden girl' had been allowed to swim in it when the family was away in San Francisco or on their estate in Hawaii. Carrie hoped it was just a coincidence that she had applied for a job on Maui.

* * *

Reunions are strange things: sometimes an outpouring of shared memories followed by the realization that there is little else to say; at other times it is as if the separation had never taken place. Carrie's homecoming was the latter.

"Your father's out in the jeep," Madge said as she continued to flail the rug. There was no 'hello', no 'how are you' and certainly no hug. But as Carrie knew well enough, her mother's brusque manner hid a warm heart even if her greeting did betray frustration that her daughter and husband should have the kind of easygoing relationship that eluded her.

"You want help preparing anything?" Carrie asked.

"There's potatoes to peel."

"I'm on it."

At that point Carrie's mother gathered in the rug and followed her daughter into the kitchen. As pots and pans were put to work and the table was laid for the evening meal Carrie felt at home.

* * *

CHAPTER 5

"Gracious God, we have sinned against Thee, and are unworthy of Thy mercy; pardon our sins, and bless these mercies for our use, and help us to eat and drink to Thy glory, for Christ's sake. Amen."

Carrie and her mother both added their Amens and Bill Holden stood up to carve the joint.

"I saw the wild turkey today," he told them as the lamb succumbed to his knife. "They were gobbling their way up the headland above the ranch house like a posse of conventioneers. They're lazy flyers, those birds. They like a bit of height so they can mostly glide to somewhere different."

"Did you see them fly?" Carrie asked. She and Jay had often trailed after them but had rarely seen them fly.

"Nope," her father admitted. "I was down below and lost track of them over the shoulder."

"They fed our first settlers," Madge reminded them. "Today no one eats the wild ones. They prefer the hormone-treated, water-injected, ready-stuffed fowl now."

"There's a trend back to what's natural," Carrie pointed out.

"The wild ones are tough," her father acknowledged, "no doubt about it. Between the two the engineered bird's the easier to eat."

"Everything got too geared to what's easy," Madge asserted.

CHAPTER 5

"Now we are starting to pay the price."

"Difficult's not a particular virtue, surely," Carrie countered.

But her mother wasn't having it.

"What I'm saying is that if folk come to think that everything should be easy they won't know how to handle those parts of life that are hard."

Bill Holden knew full well that his wife avoided what she called 'those modern contrivances' so as to be fully stretched in the life they had ended up with. 'What would I do with time on my hands?' was one of her refrains and she had encouraged her daughter to 'make something of herself' as if she had not. Only in the Presbyterian Church on Miller Avenue did she fully come alive; organizing, directing, helping.

"Are you a Doctor yet?" her father asked, anxious to change the subject. He sometimes felt guilty that he was happy in the life he had chosen and didn't want his daughter to end up as unfulfilled as he feared his wife was.

"Almost," Carrie assured him. "I am just waiting for my supervisor to sign everything off, but he lost his position a few days ago. It was the strangest thing. The research centre he headed was closed down, just like that. But I'm with the university which is separate, so it shouldn't make a difference."

To Madge, anything called a 'research centre' was suspect, especially those that trespassed on her deeply held beliefs.

CHAPTER 5

"In these hard times there are better uses of money than to spend it on questions we don't need answers to."

"Well," confirmed Carrie, "there are others with the same view. A mob attacked the Center of Applied Physics which operated out of my university and John and I - he's my supervisor - had to make a run for it. By the sound of it, they must have beaten the place up pretty good."

Her father looked worried but her mother's look was of the 'what do you expect?' kind.

"Like the incident in Detroit?" he asked. "That even earned a few lines in the local paper."

"I suppose so," Carrie said. "To be honest, I didn't pay it too much attention at the time. Research centers have been attacked in the past by groups that didn't like what they did."

"As I said," her mother continued, "when families are struggling to put a roof over their head and food on the table spending money on questions we don't need answers to is not just a disgrace, it's a profanity."

"I wouldn't go that far," her father dissented. "But you do have to wonder about priorities sometimes. There was a researcher on the National Geographic channel the other evening who had been studying primates for fifteen years, and do you know what she had worked out? That play amongst the young accustoms them to the ways of their group. Well what else would it be for? Socializing they call it. Don't we have more pressing problems to solve?"

CHAPTER 5

Carrie felt defensive.

"Science tries to find out how things work," she stressed "and that's got to be good, surely?"

But it wasn't good enough for her mother.

"Responsibility first, knowledge second, is what I am saying. When the men who taught us how to destroy the world are treated as gods, you know something is wrong."

They talked on for a while about people Carrie knew. There was a reassuring wholeness about small town life that disappeared when one slipped one's moorings and set sail on the sea of personal advantage. It was only nine o'clock when she withdrew to her old room, but she'd been driving for over four days and her eyes were beginning to close. Everything was there. The posters, her prizes, even her old bear; just as she had left them on the day of her departure for college. She'd been back many times of course but had never wanted to change anything and neither had her mother. She would get up early in the morning and join her father in the jeep as he did his morning rounds.

CHAPTER 5

CHAPTER 5

6

THE moon was so sharp it looked reachable from the cockpit, a faithful friend traveling alongside them enveloping the blackness rather than the other way around. It had been an easy flight: not quite two hours from Dulles International, named after Eisenhower's secretary of state, John Foster. Light when they left, dark now and perfectly clear. It seemed an infinite distance from the world below. In thirty years of flying he'd grown to like these moments best. Instruments telling him what he already knew. Engines sounding just as he wanted them to sound. The flight attendant came in to ask when they'd be landing. She'd had little to do. Their passenger was undemanding.

Descending through 12,000 feet Chicago appeared ahead

like a cluster of eager fireflies, each one anxious to entice, entrap and exploit. The cut and thrust, the highs and the lows, the pleasures and the pains of city life reduced to dotted lights: beyond them the blackness of Lake Michigan. He could feel it all, in a pleasurable sort of way. A person's mind tends to wander when not engaged. Keep it simple, he told himself. Call it the sweet-and-sour elixir of living and leave it at that. Once he'd have tried to spend the evening with Gena. He knew she was unattached at present. But such a maneuver had lost him one wife and brought him another and at his age why climb back onto the merry-go-round? He glanced sideways at his young co-pilot, who appeared to be half asleep, and smiled. It was his turn now.

O'Hare this is government Gulfstream 002 requesting permission to land – *002 clear direct to zulu for 2-7 left* - 002 to zulu for 2-7 left; - *002 maintain 6000* – 002, 6000; – *002 maintain 5000* – maintain 5000, 002; – *002 plan zero niner zero* – zero niner zero, 002; – *002 turn right 180* – 180, 002; – *002 maintain 4000* – maintain 4000 002; - *002 descend to 2500. Airport is 10 miles out at 2 o'clock* – descend 2500, 002; – Control, this is 002, we have the runway in sight – *002 clear for visual. Contact tower on 126.9* – 126.9, 002 goodnight; – tower this is 002 for 2-7 left – *002 clear to land where are you parking?* – apron NK1 – *is that NK1?* – affirmative, NK1 – *then take a left on alpha one* – 002, left on alpha one. Good night and thank you.

The jet came to a halt and the steps were lowered. The attendant tried to show some enthusiasm for her departing customer, but she needn't have bothered. Attorney General Stone had been watching the same moon as the captain, but his thoughts were different. He stepped without fanfare into the black Cadillac waiting for him.

CHAPTER 6

* * *

The car joined the Kennedy Expressway which reminded Stone not to get shot. He was content to forgo the immortality it brought. Both Lincoln and Kennedy had stirred up hatred but Lincoln's death appeared to be in the better cause. The Kennedy shooting was still shrouded in mystery and few people could remember presidents Garfield and McKinley, let alone why they had both taken bullets. It seemed to be as much an American citizen's god-given right to shoot his president as it was to carry the means with which to do it. At least it reminded rulers that they were not omnipotent.

There was purity in killing. He recognized that. It resolved issues that could not otherwise be resolved. But when princes became fearful of plebs order was impossible and although order was far from being the only building block of a successful state, it was its foundation stone. The 15th century Italian diplomat Niccolò Machiavelli argued that the purpose of government was to motivate citizens into sustaining a prosperous, effective polity, using fear if necessary, religion when appropriate and charm if it would work. There were, however, no simple rules. Whether prince or president, it came down to competence: the ability to read a situation correctly and act accordingly.

As they sped past Jefferson Park, the misery it contained shielded from view, he wondered if he and his President were reading the situation correctly. The country had to be made governable again. As he saw it, his job was to channel the hatred economic calamity had unleashed; to work until he was of no further use. He disliked the limelight, but he did love the power! The fear he evoked in people was like a spoonful of sugar that helped his own shortcomings go down. Being helpful to the country's most powerful man was his reason for being and he wished for no other. This was his moment.

At Northgate they left Kennedy and joined the Order Expressway crossing the Chicago River, encampments strung along it like cheap beads. His driver saw him looking. "Bad, real bad," he said, but Stone said nothing. Onto West Ohio, East Ohio and then left up Rush to East Superior before stopping outside the private entrance to the Peninsula Suite located on the 18th floor of the Peninsula Hotel. The police kept moving the bums along but like water, they kept coming back. No one could know that the Attorney General of the United States was visiting. He was expecting one guest and one guest only. Everything had been arranged by his security detail under assumed names. All the hotel manager knew was that he had no need to know. The place would not be trashed and the bill would be paid.

* * *

This would be his second meeting with Pietro LaBoucher. Once based in California, LaBoucher had run the Oakland Assassins, a notorious biker gang up to its neck in drug running, trafficking and prostitution. Pietro had moved to Chicago, partly to escape the attention of the Oakland police who seemed to be tiring of his pay-offs and partly to broaden his activities. In the febrile atmosphere that existed he'd calculated that orchestrating mob violence – encouraging it or deflecting it made no difference to him – could be a profitable line of work. He could barely believe his luck when the US government was amongst the first to call upon his services.

CHAPTER 6

Stone was oblivious to the understated opulence of the Peninsula Suite. Across its terrace he could just make out the dark void of the lake beyond the Pritzker and Kellog Schools of Management, the Feinberg School of Medicine and the Ann and Robert H Lurie Children's Hospital, all named after capitalists whose fortunes had helped endow them. He paced the room in search of the best place to conduct his meeting while the expert swept the suite one last time. One could never be too careful. Prying eyes were a menace except when they were his. People were always calling for 'open government': if they only knew! Even his President needed him to keep his secrets. The study was too intimate, the media room was a possibility but in the end he opted for the living room with its sofas and chairs. He brushed past the grand piano, pressed a key, disliked the sound and thought the instrument superfluous.

* * *

At exactly 7:30 Mr. Green – aka Pietro LaBoucher, was ushered in to have his meeting with Mr. Brown. Stone thought his team's lack of originality a little feeble.

"Thank you for coming Mr. LaBoucher."

The Attorney's sing-song greeting seemed to echo Hollywood's interpretation of the Chicago underworld more than LaBoucher's clipped reply.

"Mr. Attorney."

The gangster, for that's what he undoubtedly was, had been frisked at the door by one of Stone's men, an indignity he would not normally have tolerated.

"Please take a seat. Can I offer you some refreshment?"

LaBoucher looked at the tray on the table between them which had two glasses on it and what appeared to be a jug of lemonade. But he could see something better on the sideboard.

"Bourbon."

The Attorney studied him for several seconds and for several seconds LaBoucher studied him back.

"Of course," he said, moving toward the suite's bar. "Evan Williams?"

"Yes, thank you."

"Ice? Water?"

"No, straight."

With the balance of power resolved in a draw, the two men settled down opposite one another.

"I hope you found Detroit and New Jersey satisfactory?" LaBoucher asked.

"Entirely."

"If you don't mind me asking, what's with these research facilities? Most people have never heard of them."

CHAPTER 6

"Well they have now," the Attorney assured him. "And I hope they are about to hear of some more," he said, handing his guest a list.

LaBoucher studied it and started to count.

"That's a hundred, if I'm not mistaken."

"Indeed it is."

LaBoucher began calculating out loud.

"$500 for the organizer, $100 each for the foot soldiers - I like a hundred of those – that's $10,500 times 100 centers, so $1,050,000, plus the same again for my services, together with the $42,000 you already owe me."

Stone cradled his glass of lemon while the gangster did the same with his bourbon.

"Will you have difficulty scaling up in this way?" the Attorney wondered.

"Hell no," LaBoucher assured him. "Right now there are men who'll kill for $50. It's a tinderbox out there. I hope you boys in government realize what an explosive situation you're dealing with? Ask me to organize a march on Capitol Hill and I'll have a million men out – no trouble. Just don't ask me to guarantee that they won't tear the place and everyone in it to pieces."

"People need something to blame," the Attorney explained.

CHAPTER 6

"I think they already know who to blame Mr. Stone."

"Not who, but what," the Attorney corrected. "The belief that we know all the answers is to blame. The belief that we can leave everything to this system or that, divorced from personal responsibility, is to blame. Did you know that there are over 4,000 degree-granting institutions in this country propagating the notion that life can be learned. Skills can be learned, for sure, but not life. Life has to be experienced. The physicists are the worst. They talk about a theory of everything. A theory of e v e r y t h i n g ! Can you believe that? We have lost our sense of community. We have lost our moral core. We have abandoned God."

Pietro LaBoucher stared at the Attorney and so taken was he by these sentiments and so mesmerized by the octave of their delivery that not once had he lifted his glass.

"My mother, a good Italian Catholic, God rest her soul, used to say the self same thing," he intoned. "We were brought up to believe in family, community and God – and the priest was never able to get her to reverse that order."

For a brief moment Seymour Stone contemplated inviting his guest to join him for dinner, which otherwise he'd be eating alone, but quickly reminded himself that the abandonment of personal relationships was the sacrifice he had made in return for power.

"I guess we're done," he said instead.

"Just this, Mr. Attorney," LaBoucher said handing the

Attorney General a note detailing the accounts into which the two amounts of money were to be paid for the work done and to be done.

CHAPTER 6

CHAPTER 6

7

CARRIE could find no trace of John Franks. She needed his signature. CAP had not only ceased to exist, it was as if it never had. Dean Jimbalaya's priority was the university. Having the Center of Applied Physics located within his establishment had brought considerable kudos, but that had been thanks to Franks, its head and one of the university's tenured professors, not him. The Dean saw keeping his institution aligned to the prevailing wind as his top priority and the wind's direction had clearly changed. Nobody knew exactly what the Marjory Anhauser Theological Institute was, but it had money and he was anxious to capture a share. Unsurprisingly, none of the CAP physicists had sought shelter under MATI's wing.

Carrie drove round to John's apartment but he was no longer there. A neighbor told her that he'd left with two official looking men and that several days later his belongings, such as they were, had been collected by Bekins Van Lines. The neighbor had asked one of the drivers where they were taking the professor's possessions but the man wouldn't say although had admitted that he and his partner had a long haul ahead. "I guess it was something to do with that disruption," she'd suggested. The attack on the CAP facility had been all over the local paper. "It was just a blessing no one was hurt," she'd said. Carrie thought it best to keep hers and John's escape to herself.

Back inside the university the altered atmosphere was propagating like a bacillus and the physics department was in disarray.   However it was her friends in the social sciences who seemed most disturbed. Since their inception its practitioners had tried to emulate the rigorous clarity of natural science with its causal relationships all mathematically expressed and confirmed by detailed observation. But try as social scientists repeatedly did, the disciplines of economics, political science, business management, sociology, anthropology and the rest could not be shoehorned into mathematical equations and reduced to that fabled *theory of everything* beloved by the physicists.

It was when some academics began to argue that mathematically-expressed relationships, dubbed *artificial intelligence*, not only might push humans aside and live life for them, but – as the only antidote to the unfolding social chaos - should, that the belief in science amongst the wider public started to collapse. The instinctive although often unexpressed feeling was that as the in-charge know-it-alls had created such a mess perhaps the impeccable logic of those same in-charge know-it-alls was at fault. Carrie had some sympathy with this point of view. She knew that the apparent clarity of her discipline contrasted with the messiness of life and Jay Chandler had often teased her that while she was busy proving that 2+2=4, he would be just as busy trying to get 2 and 2 to equal 5. It didn't make any sense, but they both knew what he meant.

* * *

"You must know where Professor Franks is," Carrie insisted, but the departmental secretary was more concerned that she might not have a department to be secretary of if the growing calls in some parts of the press for root and branch reform in how physics was taught became the norm.

"If I knew I would tell you," she answered. "People keep asking me."

"Well of course they do," Carrie countered. "You are the departmental secretary; he is a professor in the department; students enrolled in the department need to know."

"Please don't take that tone with me. I have forty-two students and five professors all wondering what is going on because some hoodlums ran riot and one professor has gone walkabout. If you ask me, he should be here helping out. You could try the Dean but I don't suppose he knows any more than the rest of us. Next...."

Carrie made way for the equally anxious person in line after her who would doubtless receive the same bracing treatment.

CHAPTER 7

"I'm thinking of switching to law," the student whispered as she brushed past.

"Try theology," Carrie whispered back, only half joking.

* * *

The Dean's secretary was even more impenetrable, resisting Carrie's plea for a meeting with impressive vigor. 'She'd have to make an appointment.' 'The Dean's calendar for the month was full.' 'No exceptions were being made. The Dean was a busy man.' 'She was very sorry, but her hands were tied.' When Carrie, who had seen the Dean flee into his office like a marmot diving for cover, announced that she would sit right there in the ante-room and wait, the secretary had shrugged and said 'please yourself.' So Carrie had done just that and sat.

Waiting was clearly not catered for. There was no reading material and the one chair, of minimalist design, was functional rather than comfortable. But if PhD students learn anything on their way to that prized goal, a doctorate, it is patience: patience to find a question that has not been claimed by someone else; patience to construct a possible answer to the question that can be tested quantitatively; patience to read every book and paper, however mind-numbingly dull, that might pertain to the subject; patience to assemble a supervisory committee of three or four qualified academics sufficiently interested to pay attention to what they were doing; and patience to withstand the whims and demands of one's lead supervisor, who in her case was John Franks, an unquestionably clever man but whose opportunistic nature, unbridled ambition and carnal appetite only became fully apparent to her as her work progressed. She had managed to keep

CHAPTER 7

out of his bed by claiming a deep attachment to her own sex, but suspected this had become more titillation than deterrent. Of course she had done work for him that he had put out as his own, but that was the customary price to be paid when working with a great man. The rest of her committee had signed off on her thesis because he had said he was entirely satisfied, but so far his signature had proved elusive and now so had he.

As she sat there, Carrie started to wonder what solitary confinement might be like: a world reduced to four walls with limited human contact. She imagined herself counting the bricks demarking her cell unless they had been plastered over, in which case the cracks. A cockroach or fly would be a welcome visitor, a living companion of sorts exhibiting a freedom she could copy by moving her hand or her leg when she wanted and thinking thoughts invisible to them. 'Good morning cockroach.' 'Good morning fly.' No answer, certainly, but the secretary had been about as communicative. The tap of the lady's fingers on her computer keyboard were no more irritating than the buzz of a fly. But why be irritated at all? Did the practitioners of Zen Buddhism not seek to immerse themselves in the experience of the moment without being distracted by logical thought or language? She knew she would fail there. Mathematical equations kept popping into her head like old friends demanding to be noticed. She pictured herself constructing the ultimate equation, the one defining precisely how energy and matter worked, before realizing that even that would not free her from her imagined captivity.

With studied regularity the clock on the wall worked its way from 16:00 toward 17:00, the time when she knew Dean Jimbalaya liked to escape. Its unbending precision was her friend.

CHAPTER 7

At 17:05 the office intercom came alive.

"I'll be leaving now Janet, unless there's anything." The Dean's tone was matter-of-fact with no expectation that 'anything' would be offered.

"Carrie Holden is waiting to see you, Dean," Janet announced by way of a warning more than a solicitation for his precious time.

"I can't now, Janet," came back the expected response and she looked across at Carrie as if to say – 'well, I told you.'

There was a delay, presumably to allow his unwelcome visitor to disappear, before the inner office door opened and Dean Jimbalaya emerged from his sanctum.

He looked angrily at Carrie and muttered: "Make an appointment," before darting for the exit with her in pursuit.

"I must find Professor Franks," she pleaded. "I need his signature so that the university can award me my degree."

"Congratulations: a fine achievement. The university is proud of you." He was clearly hoping his placatory words would protect him until he reached the safety of his car.

"If you do not know where he is, can you not sign on his behalf? All the members of my committee have signed because they know he was satisfied with my work. He made that perfectly clear."

CHAPTER 7

"That's simply not possible," he insisted. "He was your supervisor and he must sign. Those are the rules."

Clearly out of breath and panting the Dean made it to the car park and was approaching his reserved place. Perhaps it was the sight of safety that caused him to lower his guard, but he stopped fleeing and turned to face her.

"Look, Miss Holden, I sympathize, I really do. But these are strange times and we must all be careful, including you. I think you will find Professor Franks in a government facility, although I strongly advise you not to go looking, unless you intend to join him. That is all I can say. Good luck."

The Dean's demeanour was a mix of fluster, concern and fear and Carrie watched him tumble into his car with just a twinge of sympathy. Her first thought was that John Franks had joined the fly and the cockroach, but that seemed ridiculous. Even if physics was becoming an object of hate, being a physicist was not yet a crime.

CHAPTER 7

CHAPTER 7

8

JAY Chandler drove the short distance from his home in Pacific Heights to San Francisco's Sea Cliff neighborhood with its views across the outer bay toward the Marin Headlands and Golden Gate Bridge. He'd read that over 1600 people had employed the structure to hasten their end since it opened in 1937 and that use of the facility was on the rise: a cheery thought on a lovely day. For once his city was free of the Pacific mist that often clung to it like a soggy raincoat and lay draped under a mantle of pristine sunshine instead.

He'd met Marjory Anhauser before at a fundraiser while she was still married, but couldn't remember which fundraiser it had been. With no children and as the sole custodian of her husband's enormous fortune she was much in demand, although the rumor was that since his death she had 'found religion' as the cynics around town tended to call it when one of their own took going to church seriously.

The address he was looking for ran off El Camino Del Mar, a road tightly punctuated by mansions. None seemed particularly old and each was designed to take advantage of the view. The driveway up to the Anhauser residence, which naturally took its name from its owner as houses of importance tended to do, making their numbers largely superfluous, was tucked into a bend and sandwiched between two adjacent properties making the house invisible from the road. He drove past the first time and had to back-track as soon as he realized his mistake. The reason for this arrangement became clear as soon as he approached the building. It sat on its own headland above China Beach with a 180° aspect few other shoreside properties could boast.

He rang the bell. An elderly maid in uniform let him in and a musty smell rushed out to its freedom in the fresh sea air. The aroma was not unpleasant but signaled that this was where an old person lived. The maid ushered him into a semi-circular living room with curved windows facing north across the bay, west over the ocean as far as the eye could see and east to the bridge. A flock of gulls were descending on something interesting in the water and the few sailboats out looked like white brush strokes. He did not notice her at first, sitting in a chair to one side, so taken was he by the view and somewhat blinded by the light.

"Take a seat Mr. Chandler." The voice drew his attention toward a diminutive woman dressed in black with a strong weathered face and the eyes of a hawk. "Can Augusta get you some refreshment?"

CHAPTER 8

"Water, thank you."

He took himself to the only chair near her, positioned so that the light from the windows fell on him and shrouded her. He had not expected an easy interview.

"So you want to run for our 14th District?" Her reed-like voice delivered the question with the directness of a lance.

"Yes ma'am, I do."

"Aren't you too young? What age are you?"

"Twenty-eight, ma'am." There were times when Southern Manners were called for, whether one came from the South or not. "I would not be the youngest."

"Washington was put in charge of one of the Virginia militia when he was twenty," she said.

Augusta shuffled in with a jug of water and a glass which her shaky hand placed on the table next to him.

"And you want me to help you with your campaign?"

"That would certainly be a great benefit to me ma'am, yes."

She watched him fill his glass and take a sip.

"This is California, not South Carolina," she chided in a more matronly than angry sort of way. "Mrs. Anhauser will do and if we get to know one another, Marjory."

"Of course ma'am, Mrs. Anhauser..." oh shit this was going badly. He was behaving like a star-struck teenager, not a Congressional candidate for the House of Representatives.

"Tell me, young man; how are you with God?"

He'd been preparing himself for some interest in his religious practices, but the directness of the question caught him completely off guard like a left hook from Muhammad Ali.

"I guess He and I get on well enough," he said eventually, which at best he could only claim was a considered answer, so slow was it in appearing.

With a nose for what was genuine, his interrogator allowed herself something approaching a smile.

"I've heard worse," she said.

"You see the thing is," she continued, "our great country has lost its way. We used to be a religious people who put God at the center of our lives. But now we put ourselves at the center of our lives. When Mr. Anhauser was building up his company his focus was on how to make things better for people, not how to make money. In the early days we had little money. Life was hard but we had each other and we had our church. We would like to have had children, but that wasn't to be. I think my husband regarded the people who worked for him as his family and I got to know a good number of them myself. Do you know how many came to his funeral?"

"No," Jay admitted, "but I read that it was a lot."

CHAPTER 8

"Over 10,000," she said with understandable pride. "Greed never drove him and people knew that. He was tough certainly, and had to be, but always fair. And if anyone in his 'family' fell on hard times through no fault of their own he made sure they were helped out."

Jay now understood why the maid was the maid. She'd doubtless be kept on for as long as she wanted to work.

"God must be returned to the center of people's lives: God, family, community – and then self. Science cannot answer all our questions, nor should we expect it to. The crisis we are in must be fixed, but it is a crisis of belief as much as it is a crisis of fact. At the height of our last calamity, brought on by a similar collapse in values, Franklin Roosevelt told us that all we had to fear was fear itself and then he set about trying to help people. Can you fight for that young man?"

"I can try."

"Then how about a scotch? I doubt water is your normal cocktail…. Augusta!"

CHAPTER 8

CHAPTER 8

9

THE Chronicle was humming with activity as usual, some of it even productive, as journalists vied with one another to put arresting stories onto virtual pages so that the advertising department could attach solicitations for things few people needed or could afford. It was beginning to be like Chicago in the 1920s when shooting followed shooting, knocking the edge off the dramatic story. Today it was the plight of the unemployed, the acts of random violence and the bodies pulled from rivers belonging to those who'd given up. What more could one say about all of that? The marriage of Miss very rich to Mr. even richer was almost becoming sought-after material.

Congress was at a standstill making it impossible for the

President to push through his program, or indeed any program. On one side, with a slender and rapidly declining majority, were the Rationalists who had run the country for a generation and championed scientific individualism. On the other were two groupings; the Nationalists for whom the nation was everything and the up-and-coming Moralists who held empathy to be the highest virtue and God alone to be the ultimate authority.

The Chronicle's editor, Sherman Parish, had started life as a Rationalist, flirted with Nationalism but was coming round to the position of the Moralists. The reasons for his shift were twofold. The Moralists were not religious fundamentalists in the sense of giving this or that practice holy status, but they did hold fast to two fundamental propositions. The first was that the universe was not some random accident but the expression of a primary truth for which the word God was as good as any other. In this they were Deists as Benjamin Franklin, Thomas Jefferson and George Washington were thought to have been. Their second fundamental belief was that the individual 'self' could only be fulfilled by engagement with the individual 'other', hence empathy from which every other value drew its legitimacy.

The second reason for Sherman's shift in political orientation was more prosaic. The Chronicle had recently secured a new majority shareholder in Mrs. Marjory Anhauser, a powerful advocate of the Moralist cause. Whether this constituted pragmatism or empathy on his part, or a blend of the two, he wasn't entirely sure. But what he and his proprietor recognized was that people's belief in rationalism had all but evaporated and that a new set of beliefs was needed before the country could become governable. While nationalism was tempting it had repeatedly proved to be a dead end with unfortunate consequences and although both abhorred doctrinaire religion, they did feel that if community-based empathy could be rebuilt the situation might yet be turned around.

* * *

The morning briefing was Parish's way of keeping his hand on the nation's pulse and his centurions in line. Liz Stoneman, the journalist responsible for scientific affairs was the first to speak.

"We need to stop hammering Science, Sherman. I don't think there's a physics department in the country that doesn't have a bunch of protesters intimidating anyone who goes in or out. It's no different from what happened to family planning clinics in the 1990s. I've been told that university enrollment in the sciences generally is way down."

"Well they are not enrolling in religious courses either," announced Paul Proctor, the Chronicle's religion correspondent.

"There's just less money around," Lesley Sharp pointed out. As the economics editor she had been tracking the collapse for months.

Sherman turned to Mark Stetz who made it his business to know about every bed ripple and cash tremor in the world of the rich and famous.

"Anything for us Mark?"

"Eighty-year-old Marty Feldman was found on the pavement in front of his apartment block early this morning."

CHAPTER 9

"So?"

"He'd omitted to take the elevator from the 18th floor."

"Not taking the elevator is hardly news."

"He didn't take the stairs either," Mark informed them in his customary dead pan tone. "The method of descent must have pleased him though because he looked very peaceful, well as peaceful as anyone can look with one of their shin bones pushed through their umbilicus."

"For heaven's sake Mark!" Liz protested

"I suppose you got a photograph," Paul surmised, barely disguising a flash of envy with his disgust.

"Wasn't he married to that twenty-eight-year-old model, Sonia Strapling?" Lesley enquired.

"Right," Mark confirmed. "She bagged him when his hedge fund Icarus Capital was the talk of the town. Apparently Feldman placed a big bet on a market bounce, but the market didn't bounce any more than he did."

"Well write it up," his editor encouraged. "Schadenfreude still sells. Can you make anything out of the grieving widow?"

"She wants $100k for an exclusive."

"Offer her $10k."

CHAPTER 9

"She'll get the hundred from one of the others if not from us."

"Well let's pass on that one," acquiesced Sherman, "but do a background piece: where she came from, humble beginnings – if they were, any other trophies along the way, you know the form."

Mark Sietz most certainly did. If there was muck to be raked he was the constant gardener.

"Can we return to science, Sherman?" Liz Stoneman pleaded. "Do you want me to cover Senator Grasser's congressional hearings?"

"Yes I do," Sherman told her. "But remember Liz, the President needs Grasser to push his Home Stabilization Initiative through Congress and at the moment he just doesn't have the votes. The Rationalists are still holding on to the fiction that their scientific management can turn this goddamn disaster around. Grasser wants to use his hearings to puncture that illusion. I don't suppose it will be pretty, but it's necessary."

"What exactly is the President's Home Stabilization Initiative," asked Mark.

"He wants to push federal money through the churches so that people can stay in their homes," explained Lesley. "It's not a bad idea, actually. The argument is that church congregations will have a better idea of people's needs than bureaucrats and that it will help to rebuild communities and reinflate the economy. The Rationalists hate it of course."

CHAPTER 9

"Where can I register my new church?" enquired Mark.

"You'd better think about joining one first," suggested Paul acidly.

"Oh, and one last thing," announced editor Parish as he was about to release his dogs of war into battle for the day, "there's a young man, Jay Chandler, running for Congress in San Francisco's 14th district. Do everything you can for him. We want him to win."

"We do?" questioned Liz.

"Yes we do," confirmed Sherman. Anyone who imagined editors did not wield power had not met Sherman Parish and anyone who imagined that proprietors were mere adornments had not met Marjory Anhauser.

"San Francisco's 14th," Mark repeated. "He must be running against Herbert Hollingsworth." The smile that accompanied this realization left everyone in the room in no doubt that Mrs. Hollingsworth was probably in for an unwelcome surprise.

CHAPTER 9

10

THE committee room was packed. Senator Arlen Grasser had finally secured agreement to hold legislative hearings around the President's Home Stabilization Initiative. Known for his trenchant, inquisitorial style the Senator from Alabama was a favorite with the networks. The press, too, were out in force. Lenses lined the chamber like hungry land crabs ready to pounce on any display of theater. Senators Holt and Davis sat on one side of Chairman Grasser, Senators Panning and de Silva on the other.

In front and at a lower level to emphasize the legislature's higher status was a table and chair for the use of each witness summoned to appear before the committee. Behind the witness table were other chairs for any aides the interrogated individual might wish to call upon. So that everyone in the room and beyond could hear clearly what was being said, inquisitor and respondent were obliged to speak into microphones. This was an arena designed for verbal combat. Words would be traded and a version of the truth established. Senator Grasser intended that it be his.

Like a million or more other people watching the broadcast proceedings, President Dukes was not entirely sure where the Senator from Alabama stood. He'd dealt with him before and knew that if anyone could move Congress on an issue it was Arlen Grasser. But the senator was his own man and could not be bought by programs for his state, although was happy to collect such payments if the desired outcome coincided with what he thought it should be. This was doubtless why his objectives often appeared opaque. Dukes had read in a biography recently that on being given the news that a famous nineteenth century French statesman had died, his equally famous Austrian counterpart had asked: 'what do you think he meant by that?' Henry suspected the same would be asked about Arlen Grasser. The man could be frustratingly inscrutable, but like the Frenchman he was pragmatic and a patriot and his offer to help right the ship of state seemed genuine.

* * *

A sharp tap on the Chairman's microphone indicated to the gathering that business was about to begin. The Senator from Alabama cast his eye around the room, pausing briefly on any part from which sound still came causing it to quickly wither under his piercing gaze.

CHAPTER 10

"I now want to call these pro-ceedings to order." Arlen Grasser surveyed the room one last time to make sure he had secured universal attention. Satisfied, he continued.

"It will not have escaped your notice that this great nation of ours is hurtin'. And when I say hurtin' I mean is hurtin' like a mountain cat caught in a snare is hurtin'. The more she pulls the tighter the wire. Every effort she makes to escape her predicament saps her strength and hastens her dee-mise. The purpose of these hearings is to ascertain if a solution can be found which our President and our Congress can put in place to ameliorate our people's great suffering."

The Chairman introduced the four senators on the podium with him, each of whom he had sparred with at some time in the past. Even if bruised from the encounter their respect for him was intact, although there wasn't one who wished to be on the other side of his inquisitorial table. Without fanfare, a bullet shaped woman with a commanding presence sat down in the respondent's chair and the committee chairman introduced her.

"Our first witness is the great Haavad economist and Chairman of our Federal Reserve System, Doctor Thelma Easterbrook. Welcome."

"Mr. Chairman," she acknowledged, her steadfast look matching his. "It's been a while," she added in a quiet voice and with a slight smile, recalling her confirmation hearing.

"Yes ma'am it certainly has. You were lucid then and I'm sure you'll be lucid now," he reciprocated. "Now Dr. Easterbrook perhaps you could tell us all where you think we are, economically speaking and what the Federal Reserve has been doing about it."

"I feel I need to go back quite a way, if the Committee will allow me Mr. Chairman," she began.

"You go back to the Garden of Eden, Dr. Easterbrook, if that will enlighten us," the Chairman encouraged with an expansive gesture that garnered a ripple of laughter.

"Well perhaps not that far Mr. Chairman, although that story still has some resonance I think. But I do want to touch on the 1980s when it was felt that our markets needed to be unshackled from burdensome government regulation which it was felt had caused a period of stagnation. Under Chairman Volker interest rates were raised to over 21% to kill off inflation which peaked at just shy of 15% in 1980. This caused a brutal recession for which our Central Bank received much criticism and coincided with the Reagan administration's tax cuts that caused the Federal deficit to balloon.

"A core part of the Reagan program was driven by what became known as supply side economics: essentially cut any regulation that interfered with market activity and growth would follow. By the time Reagan left office inflation had fallen back to just over 4% and growth had picked up to 3.4%. We seemed to be away to the races. As deregulation spread around the world international trade accelerated spurring worldwide growth and what has come to be called globalization.

"But as the new millennium got under way, the downsides of globalization and deregulation started to show. The jobs exported from our country to low cost areas abroad left behind impoverished communities and easy-going regulation allowed poor lending practices to develop, especially in the housing sector. Politicians did not ask how people on modest incomes could afford homes as long as they could claim that all was well because more and more people owned their own homes. Unfortunately they didn't; the banks did and when the mortgages could not be paid house prices collapsed and the banks would have collapsed as well if the government hadn't stepped in to bail them out.

"All this came to a head in 2008 and we have been living with the consequences ever since."

"Are you saying, Doctor, that the mess we are in now is a direct consequence of this?" Senator Grasser asked.

"No, Mr. Chairman, I'm not; not exactly. Since the 2008 debacle Central Banks have been under pressure from politicians to lower interest rates in the belief that this would stimulate growth. It hasn't worked."

"Do we know why that is?"

"I am not sure that we do Mr. Chairman."

"Well that's a mighty refreshing answer Doctor. Could you hazard a guess?"

"The backlash against globalization in this country and elsewhere prompted politicians to erect tariffs against what was seen as 'unfair competition'. This sent what had been expanding world trade into reverse. For a while our economy recovered quite well thanks to lower taxes and low interest rates but eventually the contraction in world trade affected us too. The underlying problem, I think, is that the structure of our economy is changing."

"Changing in what way, Doctor?" Senator Panning asked.

"Again, I am not sure we know precisely. Ask me in ten years, Senator, and I might be able to tell you." This stimulated some more welcome laughter.

"I'm greatly warming to this witness," drawled the Chairman. "But hazard another guess Doctor."

"The obvious things are greater automation," Thelma Easterbrook outlined, "together with a movement away from manufacturing employment to service and knowledge employment. Added to that, the rapid growth in online activity is disrupting everything from shopping malls to politics. All this is leaving entire swathes of our economy stranded as it were and generating a collapse in activity that is feeding on itself."

It was now Senator de Silva's turn to ask the obvious question.

"So what can be done?" he asked in a tone of undisguised alarm. When the high priestess of finance appeared uncertain he wondered where salvation would come from.

"The Federal Reserve can do no more. We may even have done too much. The great economist John Maynard Keynes described a similar situation in the 1930s as pushing on a string: if business can see no prospect of sales, cheap money is not going to persuade it to invest. He said then and would probably say now that only the Federal government can act."

"But we are already borrowed up to our eyeballs," Senator Holt quipped.

"And we've been spending those borrowed dollars on all the wrong things," Senator Davis added "like wars, bank bailouts and tax cuts for those who don't need the money."

"The Honorable Senator from Vermont's views are well known" the Chairman chuckled, "which prompts me to ask the key question. Could the President's Home Stabilization Initiative work?"

Thelma Easterbrook looked pensive and didn't answer straight away.

"Doctor?" the Chairman prompted.

"Well let me put it this way," she eventually began. "Getting money into the hands of those who need it must be more effective than just increasing the money supply in the way Central Banks have been doing. If our now bloated balance sheet could be reduced by the same amount as the President's program there is even an argument that the overall cost of such a program would be neutral as matters stand at present…"

"Could I ask, Doctor, for our general benefit, what you mean by 'bloated balance sheet'?"

"Certainly. Over recent years Central Banks have been

resorting to special measures in their attempt to stimulate activity, including the purchase of bonds and other assets in the open market. This increased liquidity driving interest rates down into negative territory. These bonds and other assets moved from the private sector to the Central Bank and so onto its balance sheet.

"In theory such a program could continue until the Federal Reserve owned every paper asset there was and the private sector sat on a mountain of cash, which in the current depressed environment it cannot even give away. This frankly ridiculous situation needs to be unwound. If the President's scheme could soak up some of this excess liquidity by underpinning what are the currently worthless mortgages on its balance sheet and selling them back into the market, we might begin to get out of this mess."

"So let me see if I've got this right," probed a clearly unhappy Senator Holt. "A bank writes a mortgage and sells it to the Central Bank. The mortgagor defaults rendering the paper worthless. The President agrees to underpin the mortgage reinstating its value which allows the Central Bank to sell it back into the market."

"Yes, that's pretty much it Senator," Thelma Easterbrook confirmed.

"So it is essentially a gift from the taxpayer to a man or woman who has defaulted on their mortgage?" Senator Holt persisted, showing evident disgust.

"Which is a whole lot better than a gift from the taxpayer to a bank," asserted Senator Davis from Vermont.

CHAPTER 10

"I think that takes us beyond Doctor Easterbrook's purview," observed the Chairman in an effort to keep the two senators apart. "But can I ask Doctor, for your view on the Home Stabilization Initiative's pro-posed method of implementation?"

"You mean channeling this support through the churches?"

"I do."

"Well I imagine," Mr. Chairman, "that the President's aim is to rebuild communities and values, which in my opinion is long overdue, but that is outside my area of expertise."

"Then I thank you most kindly Doctor Easterbrook. I believe we can release you," he said looking left and right in such a way as to indicate that he wanted no further questions. There being none, the head of the Federal Reserve System rose, nodded toward her interrogators and left the chamber accompanied by the sound of clicking cameras. After she had departed, Arlen Grasser suspended the pro-ceedings for lunch.

In the afternoon three witnesses were heard but they said little that caught the gathering's imagination. As Rationalists, their shared view was that although things were bad the economic system would self-correct and that the President's plan would be a waste of money. The Chronicle was having none of it though. Its banner headline the following morning read *Chairman of the Federal Reserve Supports President's Initiative* which Sherman Parish thought near enough the truth to be justified.

* * *

CHAPTER 10

The following morning was dominated by two witnesses of a Nationalist persuasion. One used the platform to castigate first the Chinese for cheating, then the Europeans for not spending enough on their defense, ending with what one could only describe as a rant against the Mexicans for allowing 'them pesky brown injuns across the border to steal American jobs.' Even Senator Grasser, who was no stranger to hyperbole himself, had to reprimand the man for his immoderate language.

The other witness did advance the Nationalist cause simply by sounding more moderate. Ours was a rich country, she pointed out, and if we spent less trying to sort out the world's problems, which to some amusement she said we didn't do very well anyway and instead spent the money on ourselves, our problems would be resolved. She had no view one way or the other on the President's initiative and although vacuously light on specifics seemed to capture the mood of the moment.

It wasn't until the afternoon that the chamber filled to hear the well known philosopher and atheist, Christian Catchment address what Arlen Grasser liked to call the God issue.

* * *

"We are honoured by your presence Professor Catchment and hope your learning can guide us into a safe harbor on this difficult issue. We do not expect you to comment on the economics of all this, but on whether directing federal funds through the churches raises issues we should be aware of. You are an a-thee-ist?"

"I am."

CHAPTER 10

"Perhaps you could start be telling us what an a-thee-ist is?"

"Certainly. An atheist is a person who does not believe in the existence of a god."

Christian Catchment was a fresh-faced Englishman, a little overweight perhaps, but possessing the sort of benign appearance that any girl would be happy to bring home to her parents, even if she might have preferred something more dangerous to go to the beach with. If one was to compare, he had the look of a slightly inflated John Denver. But as it was with the singer, his reassuring appearance belied a razor sharp mind.

"And for our benefit, could you tell us what a god is?"

"People have written books about this, but in general a god is the projection of a strong human emotion or need into some physical form that can be addressed, pleaded with, worshiped and which is believed able to cause trouble or provide benefit."

"And God, what is God?"

"All of that I have said about gods, but in one entity, an entity which is held to be the originator of existence as we know it and which embodies supreme moral authority. Various ideas about the precise nature of God have developed amongst different peoples and out of these the world's great religions have formed."

"But you do not believe in gods or God?"

"That is right."

CHAPTER 10

"But you do recognize that the idea of God has force?"

"Yes I do."

"So in that sense, God exists?"

"As a human construct, yes, but not as an entity with a separate existence."

"Forgive me professor, but how is it that God can exist as what you call a human construct and at the same time not exist? Are you saying that hu-man-ity is separable from our universe?"

"I think what Dr. Catchment was trying to say," offered up Senator Holt, "is that God does not exist outside human imagination just as ghosts do not."

"I thank the senator for that clarification but I don't think Professor Catchment was <u>trying</u> to say anything. I think he said it most clearly, in my estimation. As for as ghosts not existing, can the senator from New York be entirely sure about that?"

This stimulated the laughter Arlen Grasser was confident it would, allowing him to change the angle of his questioning.

"As you may be aware, Professor, the purpose of these hearings is not only to ascertain whether the federal government should help folk back into their homes, but whether that help should be channeled through the churches. It would be mighty helpful if you could comment da-rectly on that?"

"On whether the churches should be used in this way?"

CHAPTER 10

"Yes, whether folk needing help should get it through their churches."

"And only through their churches?" Christian Catchment asked.

"We're getting there," the Chairman expostulated in mock exasperation. "Yes, through their churches and only through their churches."

"So no church, no help?"

"I don't think the intention is that you have to belong to a church to get help," Senator de Silva elaborated, "but rather that to get it you have to go through a church rather than a government agency."

"Why not a government agency?" Professor Catchment persisted.

"Our President wants to rebuild communities," the Chairman explained, "and not have everyone tied to the government."

"Back to the Middle Ages!" muttered Catchment, forgetting that the sound system could exaggerate even a whisper.

"I rather liked the sound of the Middle Ages," chuckled the Chairman.

"Religious tyranny!" countered Catchment.

"You clearly dislike religion, Professor. But in our great land none has a monopoly – not even a-thee-ism!"

The room had been waiting for an excuse to release its tension and the Chairman's put-down triggered a rich pulse of laughter to Senator Grasser's evident delight and to the professor's clear discomfort.

"Can I quote what my good friend Professor Richard Dawkins has to say about religion?" Christian Catchment requested, as a prelude to retaliation.

"You most certainly can Professor, you most certainly can," the Chair allowed. "Although I have no idea who this Dawklin is."

"Dawkins: he is an emeritus fellow at Oxford University."

Fine credentials as these were, they did not ring as loudly in Alabama as they did in Catchment's own country.

"And on religion," goaded the Chairman, "what did this fellow say?"

"He said that a true understanding of Darwinism is deeply corrosive to religious faith. If our evolution was improbable, as the evidence suggests, the idea that God was behind the whole process – the central belief behind every religion – is even more so. In other words, the scientifically accepted process of natural selection and religious belief are incompatible."

"I think we're wandering from the point here Professor,"

the Chairman asserted. "We are talking about bringing people together under a common set of mo-al beliefs, something religions have been doing for a very long time. As I understand it, God is the concept we have chosen to embody and give force to these beliefs."

"A man or a woman does not need religion in order to be moral," Catchment countered. "And furthermore, a great many immoral acts have been carried out in the name of religion."

"Isn't the important point here," asserted Senator Davis, "that communities can only come together around a shared set of beliefs about what is right and wrong and this entails a shared understanding of how things work and a shared acceptance of the authority that lies behind the rules underpinning those beliefs? And if that isn't religion," he added, "I don't know what is."

"I couldn't have put that better myself," concurred the Chairman. "You see Professor, not evy-thing can be known by evy-one, and that fact makes belief in-de-spensible."

Christian Catchment smiled.

"Well at least allow your beliefs to change when the facts pertaining to them change," he urged.

"I think we could agree to that Professor," Arlen Grasser accepted, "but from one who has been in this game for a very long time let me tell you something: belief and power make messy bedmates. Always have; always will; making an external reference e-ssential."

On that conciliatory note the Chairman brought the second day of hearings to an end, satisfied that he had avoided having to defend the indefensible, as some religious beliefs had quite clearly become, and kept open the door to the President's initiative. He doubted he had the votes yet to push it through and hoped that his two remaining witnesses – a physicist and an evangelical - would not make the task any harder.

* * *

"Dr. Singh," began the Chairman at the start of the third and final day of hearings into the President's Home Stabilization Initiative, "I believe you worked with the Nobel laureate John Franks on String Theory, thought by many to be the final frontier of physics."

"That is correct," replied Reyansh Singh who had been interviewed repeatedly by the FBI following CAP's termination, although he had been unable to work out in his own mind what lay behind the Bureau's questions. Restricted to what amounted to house arrest, he had been unable to locate John Franks or indeed any of his other CAP colleagues and now found himself representing the Physics profession as a key witness in front of Senator Grasser's committee.

"Could you very kindly, Dr. Singh, give us a simple overview of what this String Theory is?"

"I can try, Senator."

"That's all we ask Doctor, all we ask."

CHAPTER 10

In spite of the growing popular view that the physics profession was undermining public morals by reducing the status of mankind to that of some freakish cosmic accident, all five members of the committee were curious to hear from one of its high priests. Dr. Singh took a deep breath and began.

"The idea that matter was made up out of discreet elements was first proposed by the Ancient Greek philosophers Leucippus and Democritus back in 460-370 BCE. Epicurus refined these ideas but the early Christian Church did not like his suggestion that atoms were infinite. But when atomism resurfaced in 12th century Europe through the writings of Aristotle, which had survived in Islamic texts, the French priest Pierre Gassendi proposed that the number of atoms in the universe were not infinite but finite and had been created by God."

"So science and religion were engaged in some sort of constructive dialogue?" summarized the Chairman.

"Yes, I suppose you could say that," agreed Reyansh Singh. "But it didn't remain constructive for long. As our ability to examine the natural world improved but religious understanding remained unchanged, the gulf between what was being detected and what religion held to be true grew. With such innovations as the telescope, our perception of reality slowly altered. Galileo's observations about the planets gave rise to Newton's description of gravity, subsequently revised by Einstein who explained how gravity might work, an explanation supported by later observation. While the very large was being addressed, so was the very small and the challenge became how to combine these two streams of understanding.

CHAPTER 10

"In 1906 J J Thomson was awarded the Nobel Prize in physics for his discovery that cathode rays were made of particles 1800 times lighter than hydrogen, the lightest atom, making us realize that there were smaller particles than atoms. Following on from our discovery of one of these, the electron, the workings of the atom were further analyzed to show how chemical elements were formed and electromagnetism worked."

"So science kept searching for answers," prefaced the Chairman, "while religion stopped?"

"Yes, and we are still searching. As we have burrowed down ever farther to discover what the indivisible building blocks of our universe are, we have found ourselves in a world in which elements exhibit both particle and wave like properties which limits the precision with which they can be measured. Calculations on the large electromagnetic and gravitational scale do not work at the sub-atomic or quantum scale.

"Lasers, transistors and semiconductors have all emerged out of this new understanding and quantum computers with extraordinary levels of speed and accuracy are now being developed. The challenge has been how to come up with an explanatory structure that is accurate at this sub-atomic level as well as at the level of the universe as a whole. String Theory is one such structure.

"When Einstein proposed that gravity works by warping space-time as the fourth dimension to the three we are familiar with, others started to wonder if the other fundamental forces – electromagnetism, the strong force that holds the nucleus of an atom together and the weak force which leads to its radioactive decay – propagated their effect in other dimensions so small that we have not yet seen them.

"The idea behind String Theory is that if you could look inside the sub-atomic particles we have identified – electrons, neutrons, protons, etc. all the way down to quarks – you would find a tiny vibrating filament of energy with the pattern of vibration defining the nature of the particle set just as the vibration of a stringed instrument defines its note. However the mathematics of these arrangements only works in a universe of ten dimensions plus one of time.

"When we look around at our universe it transpires that it exhibits around 20 important characteristics which have been precisely measured – the strength of gravity, the strength of the electromagnetic force, the mass of particles, etc. – such that if any were different our universe would not be as it is. So what is behind these twenty or so numbers? String Theory suggests that our universe consists of a matrix of intertwined dimensions determined by how the energy filaments inside them vibrate, precisely defining the particles and the forces that characterize our universe.

"But why should there be just one dimensional matrix giving rise to just our universe? One possible answer to this question is that quantum inflation, which is now thought to have triggered the Big Bang that started our universe, generated as many universes as there are possible dimensional sets, each with its own characteristics. So not only is life as we know it unusual in our universe, the characteristics of our universe may be unusual amongst all the other universes that exist."

Everyone in the room had been doing their best to keep

up with Dr. Singh's words and now the words had stopped. For most it had been like trying to follow an obscure fairy story. The questions wanted to tumble out. Why had the king not allowed his daughter to marry the prince before he became a frog? What spell had the jealous witch used to turn the prince into one? How had the princess's fairy-godmother managed to persuade her to kiss the frog? How easy is it to kiss a frog? Protocol demanded that Senator Grasser break the confused silence and deliver the first question.

"Well I have to say, Dr. Singh that the Latin word *miraculum* leaps right out at me. From what you have just described mankind is indeed an object of wonder and our existence is surely an amazing occurrence."

"I would agree with you Senator," Reyansh Singh acknowledged.

"So why do so many of you phys-ey-cists have such trouble with God?"

The witness knew there was no way out from this question which had been put to him numerous times by others.

"I think the theoretical physicist Michio Kaku put it as well as any of us," he answered, "when he said that 'the laws of physics are a death warrant to all intelligent life'."

"You mean that the laws that got us here are the same laws that will spell our dee-mise?"

"Yes Mr. Chairman, I am afraid that's true."

CHAPTER 10

A murmur of discomfort rippled around the hearing room.

"How is that the case?" asked Senator Davis.

"Our universe is expanding and will become a cold dark place; our sun is about half way through its life; our galaxy and the neighboring Andromeda galaxy are likely to collide in about 4.5 billion years which if nothing else will be disruptive; and if that were not enough, our solar system could be sucked into an area of great gravitational concentration, a phenomena we have called a black hole. While the laws of physics have allowed our development they in no way underpin our continuance."

"So why should we bother?" asked Senator de Silva.

"I think that's a question a lot of people are asking right now," added Senator Holt.

"I guess because bothering's better than not," shrugged the witness.

"But tell me Dr. Singh," pressed Senator Panning, "how much of this can be proved?"

"A good deal of it, Senator, but String Theory is still speculative."

"So just to be clear, Doctor," drawled the Chairman, "there are those in the physics pro-fession who believe in these strings even though their existence has not been proved?"

"That is correct Mr. Chairman."

CHAPTER 10

The answer so innocently given and of no consequence to Reyansh Singh other than it being a statement of fact, caused a stir of delight around the room equal to that in the ring when a matador has finally plunged his blade into the heart of a bull.

"Well I thank you Doctor Singh for guiding us through current scientific theology. Unless any of my colleagues have further questions, I think we can release you."

The Chairman, who sounded as if he were about to release a hooked trout back into the river looked around and was disappointed to see that one did. "Yes Senator de Silva, you have a question?"

"Thank you Mr. Chairman, I do."

De Silva, a deeply religious man who had been trying to keep up with the machinations of the physics profession on the grounds that one should know one's enemy, felt sure he had spotted an opening at least as wide as the eye of the needle through which the apocryphal camel might pass into heaven even if not a physicist.

"You have said that our universe may consist of a matrix of intertwined dimensions whose shape is determined by how the energy filaments inside them vibrate, precisely defining the particles and forces that characterize our world."

"That is correct."

"I have read that one of these forces is the repulsive nature of gravity postulated by Albert Einstein, colloquially called dark energy, which is pushing our universe apart. Its amount is one of your twenty or so numbers. In a universe with a tiny fraction more, galaxies would not have formed. In a universe with a tiny fraction less, matter would have collapsed in on itself."

"Yes Senator. That is the suggestion."

"So small initial differences can lead to very different realities?"

"I suppose you could characterize it in that way," Reyansh Singh acknowledged.

"You have suggested," de Silva continued in spite of the Chairman's growing irritation that someone else was holding the floor, "that human consciousness may be an extremely rare and unusual thing."

"It is looking that way."

"Then surely this not only puts us at the center of our universe, but at the center of a multiverse and furthermore, means that the beliefs associated with consciousness will have a profound influence on unfolding reality?"

This was altogether too much for Dr. Reyansh Singh and indeed for almost everyone else in the room and sensing that de Silva was losing his audience the Chairman stepped in to reassert his authority.

"I think this is taking us into the realm of metaphysics," adding to much relieved laughter "and physics is bad enough. Dr.

Singh, you are free to go. Let us break for lunch."

Reyansh left the hearing room relieved his ordeal was over, but wondering what career would now be open to an applied physicist. He had bills to pay and a family to support.

The rest of the gathering broke up feeling mildly disoriented. Almost everyone thought that they might just have heard something important, although no one could say precisely what it was. Even as the Chairman made his way to the private dining room for the meal he had ordered with such care, it occurred to him that de Silva could have been on to something, although like everyone else he was not entirely sure what.

* * *

Rejuvenated by the excellent lunch he had expected, Senator Grasser was feeling benevolent when the afternoon session began. Like the rest of his committee he would have preferred a nap, but his nation was in crisis and there was a job to be done. The Very Reverend Doctor Richard Preston was their last witness, someone he had every reason to believe would be supportive of the President's program. But as the Rationalist's bête noir, the preacher needed to be shown in a positive light.

"I thank you for coming Reverend," Arlen Grasser began, preferring an ecclesiastical title to that of Doctor which he felt had been debased by physicists in particular and academics in general. Where he came from a doctor either cured you which was useful or signed your death certificate which was necessary. "We have heard a good deal about the cold, cruel, godless universe we inhabit and we're hoping you can cheer us up some."

CHAPTER 10

"In the circumstances that prevail, Mr. Chairman, cheerfulness might be hard to communicate, even offensive, but I think I can offer the hope of something better."

"Well we'll settle for that," the Chairman accepted. "Now Reverend, issues have been raised which we would like you to address. As you know, these hearings are about whether it would be appropriate to channel federal money through the churches. So the first question is could the churches cope and what happens to folk who do not belong to any church?"

"Most Americans do belong to a church and I don't believe any of the major denominations would turn away a person in need. The harder part of the question is could we cope administratively? On that all I would say is that because we are active in our communities day in and day out we stand a better chance of targeting help effectively than would a state office governed by rules. I do, however, make one proviso. We must be free to solve the problem rather than be constrained by a fixed budget."

"If you want a blank check," Senator Panning asserted, "that isn't going to fly."

"Taxpayers won't stand for that," echoed Senator Holt.

"Either we solve the problem of mass homelessness senators, or we don't," retorted the Reverend.

"I believe the President's plan is to try and get folk back to where they were before the crisis struck," Arlen Grasser clarified, "so there would be an upper limit."

"So does a family from a big house which falls on hard times get returned to a big house?" Senator Panning asked, "and a family from a modest house that falls on hard times get returned to a modest house?"

"That would be my understanding," the Chairman replied.

"So aren't people going to say that taxpayers are being asked to bail out the well off?" Panning wondered.

"The formerly well off," quipped Holt.

"If inequality is a problem," Senator Davis pointed out "it is a different problem. Right now our priority must be to get things back to how they were."

"Not exactly how they were," rejoined Senator de Silva. "If distorted morality helped get us into this mess, that's something that needs straightening out."

"Which is why the President wants to go through the churches," Chairman Grasser pointed out. "But tell us Reverend, how do we stop the different denominations fightin' like rats in a sack?"

"Rats Senator?"

"Cats then. My apologies."

"In America we enjoy freedom of religion so people gravitate toward what they feel most comfortable with without the state forcing them," Richard Preston pointed out.

"That leads to some competition perhaps, but hardly fighting and competition is generally a healthy thing. You see the goal of every religion is to find a way to moral truth. Form is important, but substance is far more so."

"What do you say Reverend to those who argue that more crimes have been committed in the name of religion than on account of anything else?" asked Senator Holt.

"Are you saying that Communism is a religion, and Nationalism?"

"Maybe," Holt replied.

"And that is precisely why substance is so much more important than form," Reverend Preston explained. "Christianity challenged Judaism on these grounds, just as Protestantism challenged Catholicism. Religious form can become overly introspective even daft over time. When religious form, personal identity and power all merge that is when crimes are committed."

"How do you respond," asked Senator Davis, "to all those scientists who say that there is no evidence to support the existence of God as our creator and protector and that ultimately we are doomed no matter what we do?"

"I would agree that the god they are looking for does not exist. As eternal truth, my God is everywhere to be searched for every minute of every hour of every day – even by physicists! But that truth will not be found in mathematical equations alone because it resides in the interplay between reality and expanding human consciousness. It has to be felt. Now concerning the doomsday scenario, what I would say is this: every single one of us here today will die, but that does not stop us wanting to live rich and rewarding lives."

"An atheist would say that morality is a human construct which requires no religion and no god, however defined. What would you say to that?" asked Senator Panning.

"I would respectfully disagree," the Reverend Preston replied to some laughter.

"How so?" pressed Panning.

"Firstly I would point out that religion is merely a set of rules and procedures constructed to help individuals apply moral truth which even the moral order of the atheist would require. But secondly, and this is where the real difference lies, I would point out that Man is not some isolated intellectual entity able to pluck rules out of thin air, but part of the evolving universe.

"Even the physics profession is starting to entertain the idea that everything in the universe – or multiverse if you would prefer – is interconnected by what they are calling quantum entanglement. As such, moral truth flows from the unfolding whole, not just from men. In my language that whole is God."

"Are you saying Reverend," enquired the Chairman "that it is important that we have some reference outside ourselves to keep us straight, as it were?"

"Precisely so, Mr. Chairman, and why God needs to be returned to the center of all our lives."

CHAPTER 10

But that was not quite the end of it as Senator Holt had one final question.

"So are you also saying, Reverend Preston, that religion must not be allowed to hinder this process?"

In the gallery Abigail strained forward to hear the answer because ever since her marriage, she had listened to her husband wrestle with this very question. Could rules be picked up and dropped at will according to fashion and convenience, or were they too in some sense sacred?

"In fairness Senator, yes I am," he answered. "When something that can be learned like religious form detaches itself from moral substance which must be felt, it is our approach to religion that has to change."

The room remained silent for a while. Most of those seated had never been involved in any sort of theological discussion before. Distinctions that had blurrily passed them by had suddenly been brought into sharp focus. They could now see that truth was a living breathing thing which could only be found inside themselves, and it was uncomfortable.

Senator Arlen Grasser brought the pro-ceedings to an end.

CHAPTER 10

CHAPTER 10

11

"YES, put him through Eunice."

"Arlen, I have been expecting your call. What can you tell me?"

"I think the hearings went well enough, Mr. President. But I'm not detecting any big shift yet on the Hill. Perhaps there'll be some movement after the Congressional elections."

"A small shift to the Nationalists is the expectation I'm picking up," the President said, "but probably not enough to move things decisively. How are you seeing it?

"Much the same, Mr. President. The Rationalists are rooted to the spot frankly, dumb-founded that things have gone ass-up, and like Mr. Micawber are hoping for something to turn up. If it wasn't for the opposition vote being split between Mo-lists and Nationalists they'd be takin' on a lot more water than they are."

"Is there any likelihood of the Moralists and Nationalists coming to some arrangement?"

"Not an angel's chance in hell Mr. President. More likely the Rationalists will team up with one or the other to keep themselves in power."

"And if it is the Moralists Arlen, will that get my initiative through?"

"Quite possibly. But what I can say for sure is that if they go with the Nationalists your initiative is road-kill. That bunch has only one god in its pantheon and that's the nation - and whoever speaks for it, of course."

"Hell Arlen, the world's been down that path before!"

"It certainly has Mr. President."

"So we need to discredit the Nationalists."

"That sure would help," Arlen agreed. "But it has to tell us something that both they and some Mo-lists have it in for the pro-fessional classes."

"Tells us what precisely?" The President asked.

CHAPTER 11

"That people have simply lost faith in experts under whose watch the calamities affecting them have come. I read that the Black Death, which devastated 14th century Europe and was aggravated by the globalization of that period, weakened the authority of the Catholic Church and paved the way for the Reformation at the start of the 16th. Priesthoods enjoy privileges only for as long as people believe in them."

"That goes for presidents too, I guess," Henry Dulcer chuckled.

"Yes, and senators," Arlen Grasser laughed.

"The hatred of the Nationalists is mighty raw," the President asserted. "The hatred of the Moralists is more nuanced."

"Hatred is hatred Henry. Once let loose it's like a herd of stampeding cattle. Just has to run itself out."

"Well we need something to ease the Rationalists off their high table, Arlen."

"A branding iron up their rear end's what's required, Mr. President."

"I'm working on that Arlen."

"Well don't leave it too long, is all I'd say. This doggone geyser wants to blow."

* * *

CHAPTER 11

The Chronicle had not held back. After indicating that the Chairman of the Federal Reserve supported the President's Home Stabilization Initiative its subsequent headlines screamed *Fed sees need for moral revival; Nationalists blame woes on Mexicans; Philosopher says God and natural selection are incompatible; Physicist maintains we are doomed and part of a multiverse; Evangelist argues that religious form is less important than moral substance; Morality flows from God, our metaphor for universal truth claims minister, not from Man.*

The Nationalist press were largely dismissive of the proceedings although did make the most of Dr. Easterbrook's admission of fallibility to rubbish experts generally under a banner headline *Is fancy academic language just a cover for ignorance?* Naturally those witnesses who had derided immigration, free trade and defense expenditure cutbacks received enthusiastic support. Unlike the Moralist-inclined press who mocked physicists as well as atheistic philosophers while eulogizing the Reverend Preston, the Nationalists stayed clear of God.

It was the Rationalist organs who seemed most uncertain how to present the hearings. The Chronicle's science editor, Liz Stoneman, tried to untangle Rationalist confusion. Science, she wrote, had over-sold itself in much the same way as religion had. How the natural world worked, she suggested, was the rightful domain of science and morality was the rightful domain of religion. With quantum entanglement threatening to overturn our understanding of space and time it was just possible, she speculated, that the great schism between the spiritual and physical worlds might be healed. However that was for the future. Her readers could not be expected to grasp what had so far eluded bishops and Nobel laureates.

CHAPTER 11

But the implied scientific assumption that objective knowledge answered all questions surely fell in the face of evolutionary creativity. Knowing how something worked, she pointed out, sat within an entirely different framework to that which governed how that something should be used. Unless one believed in a fully deterministic universe in which all outcomes could be predicted, merely knowing how things worked left a rather large gap in human awareness. It was small wonder, she admitted, that an increasing number of people were becoming angered by scientists and atheistic philosophers who maintained that all questions had objective answers when it was blindingly obvious that they did not.

The Rationalist position, she suggested in her editorial following the Grasser hearings, was intrinsically confused. If intelligent life was doomed by the laws of physics as many scientists maintained, then was the mess we were in now similarly mandated? If it was, then what was the point of knowledge? And why would anything be different if there was more knowledge or if existing knowledge was better applied? If it could be different, she wrote, this implied choices in the face of uncertainty, and the only basis upon which such choices could be made was belief: belief in the superiority of one choice over another which was ultimately a moral matter not a scientific one. Even hiding behind probabilities – this course of action being more likely to lead to a positive outcome than that course – was often an abrogation of moral responsibility as well as being only pseudo science.

Her worry, she concluded, was that scientific arrogance would lead people to abandon the scientific method of enquiry into the natural world and forgo the benefits it had brought. But cerebral promiscuity, she ended by saying, was no healthier than

CHAPTER 11

any other kind of incontinence and needed to be anchored within a moral framework. She'd been pleased with that and thought her editorial had struck the right note. Sherman Parish said she'd written *a fine piece*.

But Sherman was worried. The Nationalists appeared to be making headway. Milo M Meadows III, their self-appointed leader, had a way with words. Not that it was hard to win converts by saying that the Rationalist elite had lost the plot when they quite clearly had. Even his mantras against exporting jobs and against imports that were taking bread from the mouths of working families, had a ring of common sense. And when it came to increasing defense expenditure he had the business community eating from his hand; there was hardly an industry not gorging itself at the trough of public expenditure. It was time, he thought, for something substantial on the plight of the dispossessed. Mark Stetz, his social editor, was more used to cruising the comfortable watering holes of the rich and powerful than the arid marshlands of the miserable, but needs must.

* * *

Like so many, the park had been abandoned by those seeking day-time recreation and was now home to those who could find no other. Mark wasn't sure why he had left it so late. For no good reason he had been putting it off until the cover of darkness disguised his journey into the underworld. When he left the dry empty world of street light and entered the half-light of the dell he felt strangely reassured. Behind, everything was bathed in sterile uniformity whereas here every shadow possessed a voluptuous promise of life.

CHAPTER 11

A group of boys looked his way unsure whether to rob or proposition him as he loped past like a lone wolf emitting a don't even think about it scent. From the opposite side three women emerged from a group of trees to offer their services but quickly realized he was a waste of time and withdrew back into the shadows, although not before one of the boys shouted across an insult and was rewarded with a beckoning gesture of provocative contempt. As he climbed up onto the plateau he saw the first of the makeshift dwellings that had sprung up along either side of the path; an inverted teacup of a thing clothed in scavenged sheet. On some open ground a fire blazed, sending up sparks and lighting the figures around it, some sitting some standing, each drawn in from the darkness by the flames.

His presence was noted and as quickly ignored. As he stood looking into the fire a small girl in dirty clothes approached and stared up at him. He looked down at her and she held out a begging hand. He stared back and she withdrew to a woman with matted hair, doubtless her mother, sitting on the ground a few feet away, expressionless. He studied the woman. Under the grime she had a fine face and he wondered what had brought her to this primitive state. There was doubtless a man somewhere: the oldest trade; the building block of civilization. Where had those ten thousand years gone? Was everything he knew and took for granted really so tenuous?

"Staying?"

He'd barely noticed the man who'd sidled up to him and he shrugged without turning.

"You'll have to offer something it you are," the man said.

CHAPTER 11

Mark continued to look into the flames, unwilling to break what felt like a spiritual moment with words, his stock-in-trade.

"I'm a journalist," he eventually said. "I want to write a piece on you all."

"On us no-hopers?" the man retorted.

"It might do you some good," Mark continued, "eventually."

"What we need is help right now," the man countered. "What's your paper?"

"The Chronicle."

"Makes good padding."

"Padding?"

"Under coats: helps to keep out the cold at night," the man explained.

Mark Stetz thought about that for a while. Change the circumstances and a newspaper becomes an undergarment. It wasn't his words keeping a child warm at night though, only the paper. Still, the words helped to get the paper into circulation, so he felt he could take some credit.

"Would it be alright if I spoke to some of you?" he asked.

"We're about to eat. You could join us if you wanted," the man suggested. "I'm Peter, by the way."

CHAPTER 11

"Mark," he reciprocated.

While they were talking more people had appeared out of the shadows. Old, young, families: all drawn to each other and the fire, Man's earliest mastery of nature. The scene was timeless. A cookout in the modern age or way back beyond Babylon and Thebes into the veldt of Africa: people coming together for comfort, safety and companionship.

"Everyone, this is Mark," Peter announced. "He's a journalist."

The introduction need hardly have been made because no one seemed much moved by it, save for the girl who'd first approached him. She got up from where she'd been sitting next to her mother and approached him holding out a slice of bread. He felt a pang of embarrassment that he'd ignored her begging hand.

"We can do better than that Amy," the man who was Peter said.

"Yours?" Mark asked.

"No, Fay's over there," he said pointing toward the woman with the fine face and matted hair. "But I'm with the girl's mother now. Come and sit with us."

Space was made. There seemed to be concentric circles around the fire. Fay, Peter and little Amy were part of the innermost circle, perhaps denoting a higher status or just an early arrival. There were strands of conversation here and there as people offered up food they did not need and worked out how best to open the cartons and containers they had scavenged.

"Is the Food Stamp program not working," Mark asked.

"Pretty much, but without kitchens much of what we can get is not easy to use," Peter explained. "So if a restaurant throws out something we can use, we don't turn it down."

"Do you mind me asking what you did.." and then he paused unsure how to put it, "… before all this?"

"Not at all," Peter answered. "I was an accountant. Without work I couldn't meet the mortgage. My wife left me to stay with her parents out east. I ended up here and took up with Fay. She was in human resources. Her husband was a banker until things went wrong and he became a statistic."

The man's tale was recounted in such a matter-of-fact way he could have been reading from the Old Farmer's Almanac. There was no bitterness. No self pity. But the woman had a look of cold anger. Perhaps Peter had discovered an unexpected freedom while his new partner had unearthed only shattered dreams. The girl handed Mark something wrapped in a sheet of paper. It was a bun of sorts and its wrapper the front page of his paper. That put things into perspective. A congressman and his challenger smeared in catsup.

"I've seen him," Peter said noticing Mark's greater interest in the print than in the bun. A vigorous Jay Chandler was positioned next to a jaded looking Herbert Hollingsworth, indicating the Chronicle's clear preference.

CHAPTER 11

"Which?"

"The old guy," Peter answered.

Mark noticed Fay staring at his well polished Gucci shoes with undisguised contempt. They were doubtless the jarring symbols of a past life. He spotted some dirt on one and tried to flick it off but failed causing the girl, who was watching his every move, to smile.

"He's a regular with the boys down below," Peter continued. "It's pathetic really. He thinks he's got them but actually it's the other way around. If they saw this and put two and two together I wouldn't fancy his chances. But luckily for him no one round here is much into paper reading."

"You mean you've given up on the outside world?"

"Well the outside world's given up on us so I think that's fair."

Mark had heard rumors about Hollingsworth, but this was just what he needed. Two birds with one stone. His descent into hell was proving unexpectedly enriching.

"So how bad is it?" Mark asked. "I mean up here?"

"Oh it's bad alright," Peter answered. "But bad's relative. We are building a community: looking after one another. Frankly I feel better about myself than I have in a long while."

"Before I was just going through the motions," he

continued. "Working, earning, spending on the 'good life' but something was missing. Only when all that came to an end and my wife left did I realize what it was: necessity – the need to work together to survive. I suppose war is a bit like that. I miss some of the creature comforts, of course, but not that much."

Mark thought Fay's sullen look indicated she had not yet been born again in the way Peter had.

He stayed for an hour or more and gradually others joined them. What became apparent was how ordinary everyone was: one minute a butcher, a baker, or a candlestick maker and the next minute off the cliff into the abyss. The worst affected were those without a practical skill – the analysts and other high priests of the modern economy. On that score the nursery rhyme rub-a-dub-dub about three men in a tub was slightly wide of the mark. The butcher would surely be the last to go and even the candlestick maker might find himself back in fashion. But everyone in a tub out at sea seemed apposite.

On his way out of the park he stopped to talk to the boys. Initially they thought they had a customer but as soon as Mark described what he was after, realized that something better was on offer: intrigue as well as hard cash. The values of the over-world had readily migrated to the under-, unadorned by any pretense at nobility. Their spokesman said he would have to clear it with a vague 'somebody' but reckoned it would be OK. Peter might have been running his commune but a different breed of individual was clearly running the boys and doubtless the women too, and much else besides.

Back in the office he wrote up the piece under the title

CHAPTER 11

It could be you. The quality and punch of his essay, even without the salacious stuff, surprised him. It was a human interest story from a heart Mark Stetz had forgotten he had. As surprised was Sherman Parish, gossipy innuendo with a slathering of entertaining bitchiness being his social editor's customary style. Mark took the editor's 'I hope you're not going soft on me' as half compliment, half warning, but was confident Herbert Hollingsworth would put paid to his concern.

* * *

Henry put a call through to his Attorney General. Congress would likely stay gridlocked after the elections with any gains to the Nationalists being matched by those of the Moralists, leaving the Rationalists still firmly anchored to the fence.

"That's him on the secure line now, Mr. President."

"Thank you Eunice.....Seymour, are we making any progress?"

"Frankly I am not sure we are Mr. President. The Nationalists are matching us toe to toe. Milo Meadows wants your job and is not encumbered by God, if you'll forgive me for saying so."

Henry knew Stone was not a religious man and had sometimes wondered how the ecclesiastical dirt-shovelers of the past had managed to square the circle.

"After Senator Grasser's hearings I felt there was an increase in public revulsion against scientific arrogance."

CHAPTER 11

"Quite possibly." Stone's almost melodious voice could convey meaning through a slight shift in register. "The trouble is Mr. President you and the Rationalists are in power and Meadows can promise."

"Jesus Seymour, if I had the power I'd just push my program through."

"I know that Mr. President. But what matters now is which way the Rationalists jump: toward the Nationalists or to the Moralists. Discrediting them is not enough. It's the Nationalists we need to go after."

"That's what I'm being told," Henry admitted. "Any ideas?"

Stone had heard disturbing rumors that LaBoucher was playing both sides of the fence, but didn't want to trouble the President with that until he was sure.

"Another difficulty we have Mr. President is that many of the people who would benefit most from your program have dropped off the electoral map. They have simply given up on politics and one can't blame them. This means we are preaching to the haves, not to the have-nots, and they are worried about maintaining order and the expense of your program. This is playing to the Nationalists."

"So we have to make them more frightened of what the Nationalists will do than of what my program will cost."

"That's how I am seeing it too Mr. President."

CHAPTER 11

12

CONGRESSMAN Hollingsworth slipped out of the house in a state of excitement. His wife had left for a few days to stay in their apartment on Fisher Island. Like everyone on the little island, dredged from earth surplus to the development of Miami Beach, they were worried about the effect of rising sea levels on Florida real estate. But Americans were still generally of the view that weather patterns were a force of nature to be adjusted to rather than being a consequence of human development. His bêtes noires, the Moralists, were trying to persuade people otherwise, but his electoral message *why stop progress?* appeared to be resonating well.

He didn't know much about his young challenger other

than he was a scion of the wealthy Chandler family and that this was the lad's first run at political office. His campaign manager did not seem too worried and so neither was he. Most of the papers were behind him although the Chronicle had become less than helpful ever since Marjory Anhauser had sunk her teeth into it. All this anti-science talk and stuff about God baffled him. Hadn't science brought the world such bounty? As for God, what on earth were the Moralists talking about? He and his wife attended church but his congregation for one, did not want to become involved in doling out taxpayers' money to all the no-hopers currently littering the byways. If they had made a mess of their lives, that was their fault.

The Nationalists did not seem to be making much impression in his district, which was a pity as they might have cut into the Moralist vote. His party was up against it certainly. Things were bad, that was obvious, but there were natural reasons for this. It was up to the Rationalists to stand firm and allow market forces guided by scientific management to work their magic. Government was not a moral exercise: morality was a personal matter. If morality ever did become government business he was sure the country would end up back in the dark ages as a theocracy.

He parked the car some way from the dell out of sight of the cameras that peppered the city euphemistically now known as the street police, lauded by the in-work as their safeguard against unwelcome incursions from the down-and-outs. He'd read Mark Stetz's piece in the Chronicle *It could be you* and thought it more likely to send shivers down the spines of his natural voters than evoke compassion and make them doubly determined to keep the hoards at bay. As he saw it, one big plus about hard times was that it incented those in the darker parts of the service economy to take greater care of their betters.

As he walked toward the park, his coat drawn tightly around him, he felt an almost overwhelming sense of excitement. Every part of him was focused on the moment of abandonment and pleasure which lay ahead. He knew that what he did entailed risk, but rather than dull his desire it increased it. Like a child walking on a wall edge the act demanded all of his senses, burnishing into oblivion the compromises, half-truths and sheer boredom that colored his daily life. For a few moments he knew he would feel supremely alive, free of all thought, wrapped only in sensation, like a soldier in battle poised between life and death.

* * *

"Where the fuck's Baby Face?"

The boys had seen him leave the glare of the street light and enter the park. They knew it was him. He was a regular. He was the one the newspaperman had been interested in: the newspaperman who had refused their offer and hadn't spent time with the girls opposite either but gone on up to talk with the tribe on the higher ground instead. If that community grew any larger the boys realized they might have to find another spot from which to conduct business. But right now there was money to make. The newspaperman had made a generous offer. Catch the dude at it and collect a thousand green. But Baby Face had the camera.

"Where the fuck IS Baby Face?"

"He's with someone, in the trees."

"Well go tell him he's on – or you go get the camera."

"He's the only one who knows how to use it."

"Then ready him AND the camera. But move it. We don't want fat man exploding on us before we've got Cecil B DeMille in position."

Rat, the boy so instructed by Queenie, the little group's pater familias, rushed over to the trees and found Baby Face hard at it, while Queenie set out to intercept fat man and keep him on the boil.

Rat more or less pulled Baby Face off a startled customer with both protesting and the customer mouthing obscenities about getting his money back. Once appraised of the seriousness of the situation Baby Face suggested Rat finish the job but in the commotion the customer seemed to have lost interest and was last seen running off in a state of undress fearing a police raid. He needn't have bothered because Queenie made a point of keeping the police sweet. Rat spotted the camera hanging from a branch.

Baby Face grabbed the camera which he had been given by the newspaper man's photo guy who'd brought it along the following evening hoping to hell he would remember what the photo guy had told him about which buttons to press and positioned himself behind a bush.

Fat man understood the drill and knew that in the trees was where he would find nirvana but was pressing Queenie for

Baby Face who he'd taken to. Queenie was doing his best to slow him, fumbling with the money and the like and offering him Rat instead. Rat could hear that he wasn't first choice and had half a mind to bite it off when the moment came which if nothing else would produce a fun picture. But Queenie was a stickler for quality control and forever reminding his team about the benefits of repeat custom. The high priests of scientific management would have been proud of him.

As the moment arrived they all started to realize that they had not given the slightest thought to how this was going to work. Cecil B., the great film director, might have spent hours, even days, setting up a shoot and there they were in the semi darkness with the cameraman behind a bush and one of the two 'stars' over-keen to get started while director Queenie tried to think of a way to get fat man and Rat into a position that Baby Face could see from his bush without being seen himself.

Once inside what that boys called their magic circle Rat got to work and fat man started to ascend into his own private heaven with Queenie in a kind of lemon like attendance uttering words of encouragement while trying to imagine how it all looked from the vantage of the bush. Meanwhile, Baby Face was struggling, wondering why he couldn't see a thing through the viewfinder until he realized he had not removed the lens cap. But even with that technical adjustment all he was able to see was so dark and so blurry that it could have been almost anybody doing almost anything.

By now fat man was in seventh heaven his head raised to the sky as if in receipt of a vision from the gods while Rat worked away diligently down below. It was only then that Baby Face, remembering something about a flash, moved a lever and pressed a button. The explosion of light illuminated the trees surrounding the stage on which congressman Hollingsworth was enacting his finest performance with Rat at his feet and Queenie standing like Sancho Panza by his side.

"Jesus," shouted Queenie, genuinely startled by the intensity of Baby Face's action. "Did you see that lightning? Is everyone alright?"

You don't get to be a boss, especially in the underworld, without a facility for quick thinking. Blinded, ecstatic and quite convinced he really had seen a vision, the congressman was happy to believe anything.

"Oh boy," he burbled in post-coital confusion, wholly blind to the danger "that really was ……." But words failed him and the best he could do was pull a ten dollar bonus from his pocket and offer it to Rat who was doing his level best not to choke.

As Herbert Hollingsworth stumbled back toward the over-world unsure what had just happened to him, but resolving that that would definitely be his last, absolutely his last visit to the dell, the three boys looked at him, looked at each other, looked at the camera and laughed.

"Did we get anything?" Queenie wondered.

"I don't know," said Baby Face.

"Can't you check?" prompted Rat.

CHAPTER 12

"I don't want to touch anything," answered Baby Face. "I might erase it."

That was only partly true. As an aspirant Cecil B. he preferred not to know in case their efforts had been in vain.

* * *

The following morning three young men plus one camera presented themselves to the Chronicle receptionist who was not much impressed by their appearance as none of them had yet gone to bed, so keen were they to claim their reward. Baby Face was in a state of nerves. He had also mislaid the photographer's card and the best Queenie could come up with was that he thought he had spoken to Mark something.

"Could it have been Mark Stetz?" she wondered although the bedraggled creatures in front of her did not look like the social editor's customary clientele.

"Yeah," thought Queenie. "It was something like that."

As lukewarm as that confirmation was, the receptionist was used to all sorts walking through the door: this was a newspaper after all, a drain down which all manner of human detritus flowed. So she dialed his extension.

"Mark I've got three young men down here. Could they be anything to do with you?"

"Yes, pretty rough," she replied to his question which seemed to be just what he was hoping for.

CHAPTER 12

"He'll be right down," she told them.

By now Baby Face was a nervous wreck as everything hung on his inept handling of the camera. "I shouldn't have said I knew how to use one," he whimpered to no one in particular.

His fragile state was not helped by Rat eulogizing over all the money they were about to take away, although this did stop when Queenie, who felt such bare-faced greed was unseemly in their present surroundings, gave Rat a death stare.

Mark almost bounded in, so excited was he by the prospect of what he was about to receive.

No sooner had Baby Face handed over the camera than his legs buckled and Queenie and Rat had to hold him up.

"Is he alright?" asked Mark holding the camera as if it was a sacred object.

"He's worried there may be nothing on that thing," said Queenie.

Mark's elation evaporated.

"You haven't looked?"

"We didn't know how," Queenie told him. "Baby here was worried trying might wipe anything there was."

Suddenly the possibility of a Christmas stocking containing no more than a lump of coal appeared all too real.

CHAPTER 12

Mark held the camera up and pressed a button as he peered at its liquid crystal display.

"Jesus," he exclaimed. "J_E_S_U_S!" he repeated.

"Well," mouthed Queenie. "IS there anything?"

On the small screen Mark could see an enraptured and trouserless Congressman Hollingsworth, half-shut eyes pointing heavenward, with Rat kneeling at his feet as if awaiting a priestly benediction.

"Oh boy," he said, but quieter now as he regained his normal composure. "So I guess you boys would like our side of the bargain?"

"That would be nice," confirmed Queenie.

"Then wait here," Mark told him. "I'll send someone down."

Suddenly the three musketeers felt vulnerable and out of place in the smart reception hall as they stood relieved of their treasure and a long way from the comfort of the dell where they ruled. None spoke. Even the receptionist ignored them as a steady stream of people came up to her desk and were efficiently dealt with. Her expensive scent did its best to shield passersby from their own arid aroma which seemed to be acting as a force field between them and the alien world they had stumbled into. After what felt like eternity a young man wearing spectacles appeared and handed over an envelope. He waited while Queenie counted its contents – twice, just to be sure. It was all there, as agreed.

The trio left as if walking on air, with Baby Face now fully recovered telling them he thought he might go into films.

CHAPTER 12

13

A respectable matronly sort of woman, who he took to be Mrs. Hollingsworth, let him into a house that was not flashy or opulent but solid and guided him into the Congressman's study. This was not the first time Mark Stetz had been the bearer of awkward news and he hoped it would not be the last. Such little pantomimes, as he thought of them, in which his job was to prevent Judy pulverizing Punch - and it was usually going to be that way around – for what he politely called 'a consideration' greatly enriched his working life. He sometimes reflected on the ethics of rescinding a threat in return for a course of action. When Al Capone made sure a person could continue his business in exchange for a payment it was considered bad. But when the government did the same it was regarded as necessary even though both government and gangster ultimately relied on intimidation to get their way.

"My husband's in the garden," the lady explained. "I know he's expecting you. He won't be long. Can I bring you some coffee?"

"Yes, thank you."

Mark was sure the Congressman would need something stronger soon enough, but coffee would do for now. He'd told the politician's secretary that the Chronicle wanted to do a profile piece on each of the candidates, so that was how the interview would have to start, at least until Mrs. Hollingsworth had finished being a solicitous hostess.

While she went off to retrieve her husband and make the coffee, Mark looked around the room. There were shelves of law books. Its occupant had been a lawyer, often the stepping stone onto the public stage. There were the usual family pictures alongside photographs of him with others more powerful. He'd even got one of himself and President Dukes, signed. The photograph he was carrying would not find its way onto any of the shelves which seemed a pity. Michelangelo had managed to display one of his great fantasies on the ceiling of the Sistine Chapel, so a little nod to human reality would surely have been welcome. But politics was no more about reality than was the great painter's depiction of God creating Adam. Blowing bubbles of self-serving innuendo was what politicians did and it was down to low-life like him to prick them.

"Mr. Stetz, it's good to finally meet you," the Congressman

announced as he floated into his study like a party balloon, extending a flabby hand still moist from the removal of God's good earth. "You have not always been kind to me."

"My paper is not a mouthpiece for the Rationalist Party, but we do try to be fair. Our readers deserve to hear your views."

Reassured by the journalist's claim to fairness and anxious to reach voters, Congressman Hollingsworth sat himself opposite Mark Stetz in a comfortable chair with a glass table between them, rather than behind his desk, in a display of intimacy intended to indicate that he was taking the Chronicle's centurion into his confidence.

"What terrible times we live in," he said as if it was a misfortune he shared. "I believe Barbara is bringing us some refreshment."

"Indeed they are Congressman," Mark agreed, but thought he should get right to his formal agenda. His informal one could wait. "Where do you stand on the President's initiative?"

"His Home Stabilization Initiative?"

"Yes."

"Laudable. Most laudable. It's a fine idea. But I don't think my colleagues in the House will vote it through."

"Will you vote for it?" Mark asked.

"Not as it stands. Going through the churches would be a

retrograde step," the Congressman claimed.

"Why do you think so?"

"Don't get me wrong, Mr. Stetz. I am a churchgoer myself. But our great Republic is built on a separation between church and state."

"So from where do you think the moral dimension of our lives should draw its strength:" Mark wondered, "from our religious beliefs or from our state structures?"

Congressman Hollingsworth glanced at his watch. "I wonder how Barbara is getting on. I'm parched."

"You enjoy gardening?"

"Yes, very much. It takes one's mind off things."

Mark suspected that most politicians were only too happy not to have to think about things, so why not a hobby that served that end.

"Ethics is becoming quite the subject in our universities these days," the Congressman noted in a somewhat oblique reference to Mark's original question.

"Do you think science can answer our moral questions then?" Mark asked.

"Oh yes," the Congressman enthused. "I am sure of it. Just look at the wonders scientific management has brought us.

CHAPTER 13

Our problem is that government has not been as rigorous as the private sector."

"Or as ethical as our various religions would have us be!" Mark asserted.

"Oh there have been failings, certainly," the Congressman agreed. "But they have not been the failings of science. It's science that will get us out of this mess, you'll see."

The study door opened and Barbara Hollingsworth came in carrying a tray. On it were two cups of coffee, a jug of milk, a bowl of sugar and a plate of cookies.

"Are these the Girl Scout cookies Barbara?" Congressman Hollingsworth asked eying up the plate with keen interest.

"Yes they are dear."

"Do you know," the Congressman elaborated, "that over $800 million is raised for the movement in a year by having the girls sell these cookies – and they are good too!"

"Pleasure with purpose!" Mark joked. "What could be better?"

"Thank you Barbara," her husband said.

"Remember you have another appointment in half an hour," she replied, long practiced in giving her congressman a well–signed escape route.

As Mark watched her go and the Congressman dive into the cookies – such a sublime scene of simple ordinariness - he found himself wondering at the conflicted nature of human existence. At one moment supporting girl guides, at another bombing some far away village for reasons of high politics; in the morning kissing a loyal wife, in the evening becoming the prisoner of a dastardly passion.

His host chattered on, oblivious to the catastrophic exposé heading his way. If there was a God, Mark thought, He would surely be endlessly entertained by our antics. As a boy he had been fascinated by the ant colony he had kept in a perspex box, until his mother had thrown it out. The passages, the egg chamber, the eggs, the sheer busyness of the creatures, not to mention the macabre pleasure he had derived from dropping a live moth into their midst and watching it twist and turn helplessly as the ants set to work. It was as if the possibilities Man had given himself far exceeded Man's ability to handle them. Perhaps we did need God, he was starting to think, just to keep us in line.

"Congressman, I am afraid I have some bad news," he announced when he was sure they would not be disturbed.

"Another poll? I was doing OK in the last one."

"No, not a poll," Mark replied as he extracted the photograph from his inside pocket and slipped it across the glass table.

Herbert Hollingsworth leaned forward, stared at what was now in front of him and turned white. Mark could see beads of sweat breaking out across his forehead.

CHAPTER 13

"Where did you get this?" he eventually asked. "It's disgusting. It's a fake of course, to discredit me."

Mark could see that the previously confident man in front of him was shrinking into his chair. If he had been able to disappear he surely would have. The sound of the carriage clock on the shelf next to an unread copy of John Bunyan's Pilgrim's Progress given to him by a local church whose charity appeal he had supported ticked and tocked like the sound of an executioner's metronome marking the moments to the appointed hour.

"Who else knows?"

The Congressman's words were weak. The puff had been knocked right out of them. In his heart the politician had known that years of risk-taking would one day catch up with him, but he had somehow hoped that day would never come.

"I think we have it contained Congressman," the Chronicle journalist disingenuously replied. "But who knows what might come out of the woodwork if you continue to run."

"I see."

He had thought of making this his last term, but one gets used to the trappings of power.

"If you were to endorse your opponent," Mark Stetz suggested, "I think we could guarantee that this business would go no further."

CHAPTER 13

The Congressman allowed himself a weak smile. He knew how power worked. He had played the game himself many times.

"I would like a positive political obituary in your paper. I <u>have</u> done some useful things."

"I think we could manage that," the journalist agreed.

"Well then Mr. Stetz, we are done. Please see yourself out."

On the way Mark passed Barbara Hollingsworth arranging some flowers from the garden in the hall.

"Did you get everything you needed?" she asked.

"Yes I did, thank you," he told her and felt a pang of guilt as he stepped out into the street and inhaled the evening air. Did she know? Would she know? Could her husband stop doing what he did? What drove him to it? Did any of it really matter? All interesting questions but they were not his concern.

* * *

It couldn't have been more than ten minutes after the newspaperman had left, following the flowers and a visit to the kitchen to make a start on the evening meal, when Barbara Hollingsworth returned to her husband's study. She found him still in the chair where she had left him but slumped slightly to one side. He had had a massive heart attack and was quite dead. On the floor beside him was a photograph. She picked it up, looked at it and quickly took the monstrous thing to the kitchen sink where she set it alight, washing the ash down the waste.

CHAPTER 13

She then returned to the study and sat opposite her Herbert in the chair Mark Stetz had used just looking and thinking about all the good times they had shared. She wasn't angry, just sad that his habit had finally caught up with him, a habit it had been beyond her to break. In every other way he'd been an exemplary partner. They might not have shared physical intimacy, an aspect of life that repelled her, but they had shared everything else: the campaigns, the political highs and the political lows, the successes - when the lives of some had been made a little better, the failures - when a good idea had been shredded by political compromise.

She waited for as long as she decently could before calling an ambulance. After that he would no longer be hers. Two days later an unexpectedly flattering piece appeared in the Chronicle, in which he was quoted as saying that the President's Home Stabilization Initiative was laudable. As it happened, she thought it was too. Even his young challenger had said some nice things. What a game it was, the game they all played.

CHAPTER 13

CHAPTER 13

14

GOD THIS DAY flags fluttered everywhere. The sense of purpose inside the American Airlines Center stood in stark contrast to the vapid swirl of disconnected listlessness outside it. Dr. Richard Preston waited in the shadows for his cue to ascend the stage. Whipped up by cheerleaders, the chant *GTD, GTD,* reverberated around the walls imploring its object to help solve the problems the chanters alone could not solve but that He, with their unqualified support, could and would.

The 15,000 or so inside the hall were experiencing a kinship, a shared identity, a mission, that was absent from their lives, save at concerts or games, which were now infrequent and few could afford. Dallas, a city of 1.4 million people, had been hard hit. Unemployment was over 20% and the Texas state budget was in tatters. The 36 acre Reverchon Park had become a tent city, home to over two thousand families, refugees in their own land.

The Nationalists had held a rally the previous week in the Kay Bailey Hutchison Convention Center which had drawn a respectable crowd of 5,000. Their leader, Milo M Meadows III was interested in those who were still employed rather than in the down-and-outs, as he called them, calculating that they were more likely to vote and send him to the White House in place of President Dukes. As an added incentive he had arranged for his 'toughs' to engage in some inner city looting which he then blamed on 'bad elements' from the various camps around the city.

His message was always the same: improve law and order, which endeared him to the police; strengthen the military, which endeared him to the generals; and foster economic growth over what he called those touchy feely green issues; all of which played well to those whose votes he sought. But his trump card was always to demand – yes demand, a tough trade policy that 'puts our great nation first'. Mary Dukes tried to stop her husband watching clips of these speeches on the television for fear that doing so would induce in him a heart attack. "That goddamned liar," he would habitually grumble. "He has not got one policy that would get us out of the hole we are in."

As he watched his excited audience from the wings, Richard Preston wondered how many had come to enjoy the free food that was on offer, courtesy of the Bill and Marjory Anhauser Foundation. He smiled to himself remembering that when the crowd followed Jesus to Bethsaida after the beheading of John the

Baptist by Herod of Antipas, the fare had been more meagre: just five loaves and two small fish. But now just as then people needed to be looked after, a simple fact that the neo-liberal Rationalists in government had lost sight of.

At his cue, Abigail, standing beside him, whispered "good luck" and he bounded onto the stage and into the glare of his followers like a thousand performers before him anxious to reflect the energy they gave.

GTD, GTD, greeted his arrival and continued as he embraced those around him with his presence. Gradually the sound subsided in response to his gestures indicating that it was enough. When he was sure of their attention he began.

"I want to start with part of a prayer attributed to a 16th century sea captain, privateer, slave trader, naval officer and explorer. He was regarded by the Spanish as a pirate and by the English as a hero. His name was Francis Drake and he was all too human.

> Disturb us, Lord, when
> We are too well pleased with ourselves,
>
> Disturb us, Lord, to dare more boldly,
> To venture on wider seas
> Where storms will show your mastery;
> Where losing sight of land,
> We shall find the stars.

"Apart from the sound sentiments expressed you might think it odd that I have chosen to start with the words of a thief, a killer and a trader in slaves. He was all these things, but he was also brave, skilled, and not afraid to pitch himself, body and soul, against the greatest power of his age. No, that was not our United States, not Russia, nor China, but Spain. A reminder that it is as well to look at the world from the standpoint of the powerless as well as the powerful: you can never know into which camp you will fall. But more than this, I picked him because he was a human being with strengths and failings just like our own. I picked him because he recognized his limitations in the face of God.

"So what is the God who has brought us all to this great stadium today?"

Echoes of GTD, GTD rippled around the tiered rows of people anxious to hear his answer.

"Well I will tell you what that God is not. That God is not the old man sitting atop the universe derided by physicists…" Sounds of 'right on' and other notes of approval reverberated around the hall. "That God is not a supreme being who started the universe and holds its future in his hands…" The sounds of approval were still there but were less intense this time. "That God is not some personal talisman we can consult at will and from whom we can solicit favors…" This time the sounds were more of disappointed confusion than of approval. Richard Preston knew he would now have to gather his flock in.

"So what **is** God?" He paused for impact before continuing. "God, quite simply," he said "is e-v-e-r-y-t-h-i-n-g." A few brave souls tried a 'Halleluiah' more because they felt they should than because they knew what he meant.

CHAPTER 14

"But let me put this in a different way. Let us assume that the physicists do, eventually, come up with their beloved 'theory of everything', will that stop the clock, be the end of history, the end of time? Hardly," he said with a faint smile. "It won't even be like learning the rules of chess without knowing how to play the game."

Some thought they understood a glimmer of what he was saying and omitted a positive sound

"It won't be like learning the rules of chess without knowing how to play the game," he repeated "because the nature of the game itself will change. You see, my friends, we live in an innovative universe and while its rules can be learnt, its outcomes are – in part - for us to create.

"If you threw all the notes a piano can play up into the air would they fall down in the order of a symphony? It would be possible, I suppose, but highly unlikely. And why is that? It is because we are part of an interacting whole in which everything in it plays off everything else to form some sort of coherence. But this is not a static coherence it is a dynamic coherence that tends toward the complex and beautiful. It is up to us to learn its rhythm so that we too can create what is beautiful and avoid what is ugly.

"God, my dear friends, is the word we use for the rhythm that runs through everything. If we are in accord with that rhythm the relationships we create will be life enhancing; if we violate that rhythm what we create will be life destroying.

"And where does religion fit in to all of this? Well first

and foremost religion is about rules of behavior; how you and I should act toward each other. These rules of behavior gain their legitimacy by being in accord with the rhythm that runs through all things. People called priests have come to translate these rhythms into rules for us, and power structures, stories and identities have been built around them.

"But as we know only too well, religious hierarchies have often become self-serving, rule-bound power structures, something the founder of the Christian Church objected to."

Someone shouted 'right on' but his call was not taken up.

"Unfortunately the Christian Church succumbed to the same vice and only when we imbued secular institutions with moral authority and allowed freedom of religious practice, was this bad habit broken. But this gave rise to a new bad habit: that of imbuing nations rather than religions with supreme authority and much blood has been spilled because of it.

"Our movement aims to go beyond individual religions and individual nations. Our guiding principles are compassion for individuals and empathy with the whole. We simply cannot go on riding roughshod over the lives of men and women while abusing our planetary home, all in the name of a progress which is underpinned by some rootless thing called scientific management."

This struck a chord and the crowd responded with eager sounds of approval. But the preacher held up his hand.

"Contrary to what has been written about us," he

continued, "we are not against science, we are not against market economies and we are not against nations. We are simply against assuming that any or all of these should be allowed to function outside a moral framework that emphasizes compassion for individuals and respect for the whole. We call that moral framework, that rhythm of life, God."

From the rising upswell of approval around him, he knew he had regained his audience.

"The crisis that has affected so many of you here this evening arose because of an arrogant belief that we had created a perfect political economy and that all we had to do was sit back and let it carry us forward to ever-increasing prosperity. **How wrong those who thought like that were!**"

The urge to blame was not an emotion the Reverend Preston much admired, but it was a powerful one which had a time and a place. Now, he calculated, was its time and this was its place and his followers rose wild in agreement as if exorcising their frustrations and letting him know that they were his. 'Tell us what we must do', they seemed to be pleading and we will do it: just give us the word.

The crowd wanted to express itself and the Reverend was happy to let it do so for a little longer, but as soon as he sensed signs of exhaustion he held up his hand to quieten his supporters.

"Now I am very pleased to be able to tell you …", he began and then repeated as the last of the adulation died down, "… pleased to be able to tell you that we have a very special guest here with us tonight." Slowly calm and expectation took hold and the noise in the hall abated. "Can I ask you to give a very warm Texan welcome to the President of our great United States, President Henry Dukes."

From the side the tall imposing figure of the President strode on to the platform, a man one could more easily imagine riding horseback across the Wyoming range than stalking the corridors of power in the capital. Richard Preston stood aside so that the President could command the stage.

"It is a privilege to be able to talk to you good people in this fine hall this evening," the President announced turning to his host. "I would like to thank Dr. Preston for affording me this opportunity. Only a little over a year back, Reverend Preston and his lovely wife Abigail joined Mrs. Dukes and myself at the White House for a meal and it was, I can tell you, an inspiration. If anyone can turn despair into hope and cynicism into constructive action it is surely Pastor Preston.

Sounds of agreement came from every part of the arena.

"Now you may have heard that I have been trying to get my Home Stabilization Initiative through Congress. If passed, this bill will start the process of rebuilding our broken communities. Families will be helped back into their homes which at present stand empty with dilapidated *For Sale* signs attached to them on the orders of banks that have repossessed them and stand to receive nothing.

"The Rationalists in Congress believe things will right themselves and that our economic system is fundamentally sound. You and I know that things will not right themselves and that our system is not sound. Even those inclined to think that just possibly my initiative has some merit object to the idea that our churches should be the bodies charged with directing our federal money to the dispossessed. So let me tell you why they are wrong.

"Our system failed – you good people are testament to that – because decision-making was put on autopilot without any moral override. So long as all was well for those at the top, no one thought to pay attention to the damage being done to those at the bottom. But now that the floodwaters of pain have risen to lap at the ankles of increasing numbers this complacency is being eroded.

"The Nationalists are telling us that it is our country against the world and that salvation will come through greatly increased defense expenditure and a curtailment of imports so that our own labor is used to make what we need. It's a beguiling message. But think it through. What use are armaments unless we plan to go to war? The making of them will keep some of us busy for a while, but then what? Sure we could keep everyone busy by paying them to dig holes in the ground and then paying them to fill the holes back in. But how would that augment our quality of life?

"Now as for self-sufficiency, sure we could go back to the time when a family had a cow and a plot of land and struggled through from one year to the next living off the few things they could grow and the animals they could tend. But we didn't start trading with our neighbors because it hurt us. We started trading with them because it enriched our lives. Trade, however, increased our dependence on one another, but as the circle of our interdependence grew, so did our prosperity. What has gone wrong is not trade but the abandonment of any moral constraint over how trade is conducted.

"Science has turned us away from religion because many religious beliefs were constructed hundreds, sometime thousands of years ago and are bizarre to our modern ear. But all the major religions share one thing which is not bizarre: a concern about how we should behave one with another and fit into the whole of which we are a part. This is the morality we have failed to apply and which draws its authority from something outside ourselves which we call God."

This was music to the ears of many listening and they showed their appreciation.

"So what can you do? Now I know that many of you – most even – must feel that politics has let you down and is no longer worth bothering about. Well sometimes change is mighty slow. In spite of everything I urge you to continue supporting this GTD movement, and when the opportunity arises to get out and vote for Moralist candidates. They may not all be saints, but for now at least they are pointing in the right direction. God bless and thank you for listening."

The applause was more than polite; it was enthusiastic but it was respectful. This was their President after all and most had come no closer to the holder of that office than their television screens in the days when they had televisions to watch.

Richard Preston came back onto the stage leading a further burst of applause for President Dukes who waved, shook hands

CHAPTER 14

with the Reverend Preston, turned and was hustled away by his minders to the bullet proof car outside that would whisk him off to Love Field where Air Force One was waiting to carry him back to the capital.

As the applause wound down like an engine deprived of fuel Richard Preston waited for Henry Dukes to disappear from view before turning to the microphone.

"Well folks that was an honor," he said. "So it's up to each of us not to let our President down." He glanced at his watch and at his notes: they were on schedule. "Now for the moment you have been waiting for," which for many was indeed the case, "and with our thanks to the Bill and Marjory Anhauser Foundation," which the preacher thought would have to do for grace, "victuals are being served in the ante-rooms."

CHAPTER 14

CHAPTER 14

15

THE reception was in full swing. Milo M Meadows
III was keeping an eye on proceedings from one corner like a
medieval monarch surveying the members of his court at play.
The Jackson Westin, just four blocks from the Mississippi
Governor's mansion, was used to these affairs at which the state's
up-and-coming and its leading lights burnished their authority
and displayed their commitment to whatever cause was most
likely to keep them in power. The city was not large, with less
than 200,000 inhabitants. Although the metropolitan area was
predominately white, the great majority of inner city residents were
black and it was on them that the depression had fallen hardest.
In the banqueting hall there was not one African-American face
to be seen and the talk was about how to keep 'the colored' from

running riot, a cause dear to Nationalist hearts.

The land around Jackson had once belonged to the people of the Choctaw Nation until European settlers took it off them under guise of a treaty in 1820. But even that wasn't enough for the new arrivals. Ten years later the Choctaws were forced to vacate all their lands east of the Mississippi, the mighty river that carried Indian traders and then French ones from the Great Lakes in the north to New Orleans in the south, eventually becoming an industrial highway from Minneapolis to the Gulf of Mexico used by river boats to transport the families, adventurers, opportunists and hucksters written up by Mark Twain and Herman Melville to their futures, unaware of a past they had buried.

The city missed out on the Mississippi's bounty, being located on the adjacent Pearl river and had stayed small. It had even started off with a different name: LeFleur's Bluff after a French trader, until it was renamed to honor America's seventh president, Andrew Jackson, and commemorate his victory at the Battle of New Orleans in 1815 over the British who were already somewhat stretched at the time trying to deal with a self-styled French Emperor four thousand miles away.

The Confederacy finally abandoned Jackson in 1863 and Union soldiers burnt the place to the ground leaving only a forest of brick chimneys. While freed black slaves fled north in search of a better life and the state struggled with reconstruction and the development of its constitution, those that remained were repeatedly disenfranchised by whites anxious to maintain control. Even after the Civil Rights Act of 1964 and Voting Rights Act the following year, whites dug in and the Ku Klux Klan set about terrorizing blacks and those who supported them. An uneasy

CHAPTER 15

peace gradually took hold between the two communities but old animosities ran deep and Milo Meadows knew how to play them to his advantage.

The Police chief was there of course, a burly man with a ready baton and a high conviction rate when it came to Americans of color, as was the state governor who refused to sanction any action by the National Guard unless it was directed against 'those varmints', a cohort never specified because in polite society there was no need to.

The mayor was in attendance, a useful fool with a drug problem and penchant for gambling. Anyone with power and money could bend him to their will and the city's black hookers regularly took him for everything he had to offer. This was in spite of the police chief's half-hearted attempts at scaring them off, an uncharacteristic lack of rigor only accounted for by his own interest in their services. On the positive side of his balance sheet the mayor was charming and very good company, but it was generally assumed that he would end up at the bottom of the Pearl River one day. The city had a history.

When alcohol was outlawed in Jackson during the long prohibition period between the 1920s and '60s, illegal gambling, drinking and prostitution flourished on the east side of the river under the covert protection of certain city fathers. Known as the Gold Coast on account of its thriving black market economy the area fell into decline after 'sin' was legalized, in spite of objections from the temperance movement and its commercial beneficiaries. The area did have a brief period of legitimate economic excitement. Oil and gas were discovered close to Jackson in the 1930s but enthusiasm had to be tempered when

CHAPTER 15

the oil was found to contain high concentrations of salt which seemed to reflect the city's split personality.

Much of this Milo Meadows did not know, but what he did know was that there were countless communities across his nation just like Jackson which felt abandoned by a Rationalist elite whose eyes were fixed on the international arena and the prestige performing in it brought them as well as on the wealth that poured into their pockets from the laissez-faire system they nurtured. Methodically his aides were identifying these economic orphans so that their candidate could show interest and tie them to the Nationalist cause.

"Senator, it's time for the photographs."

"OK Anthony. Let's get this over with."

Milo Meadows followed his aide through to the room set aside for the charade. In the adjacent ante-room various members of the State Government who had been carefully selected for the honor of being photographed with the Nationalist leader were milling around clutching glasses of wine and dipping into the canapés on offer.

Anthony was nothing if not efficient. He positioned the senator in front of the national and state flags that had been set up and gestured to his colleague to start sending the fortunate through.

The head of Veteran Affairs was ushered in to receive a warm greeting and a firm handshake - SNAP – before being guided across into the banqueting hall to rejoin the party. The heads of the State's parks, pensions, fire service, public health, environment, energy, indeed a steady stream of officials all followed, one after another, with Anthony priming the senator about each: name and notable achievements if there were any, so that the moment felt personal. It was a slick production line not unlike the branding of cattle: once marked the individual was deemed to belong to the Senator.

You could measure the political usefulness of an individual by the amount of time the Nationalist leader gave them. The Adjutant General whose task was to oversee the National Guard was favored as was the head of the State's police. Education and Health were given time, more because of the size of their departments than because of their political utility. Most were in and out as fast as the camera could shutter, but would still go home with a warm glow knowing that they had touched power and would soon receive evidence to prove it through the mail.

Last, but far from least, came the turn of the State's attorney general, lieutenant governor and governor, each themselves well practiced in the art of political stroking. For these worthies it was less about the photograph than about the shared joke and the acknowledgment of whatever special interest they had that the candidate would lubricate in return for their support. This was politics in the raw, a politics that had changed little over the centuries and which the Italian had written so well about at the start of the 16th century in the Florentine republic.

When the ante-room was empty and only the Senator and his aide were left in front of the flags, there was a moment of relief.

CHAPTER 15

"Have you managed to arrange the meeting I asked for?"

Senator Meadows's question seemed matter of fact. The cameraman was too busy to hear it gathering his equipment and checking that he had the name of the person in the candidate's office who would be sending out the photographs, each numbered to tie in with the list: it wouldn't look good to send State Parks to Motor Vehicles.

"He arrived twenty minutes ago," Anthony reported. "I'll take you to him."

Milo Meadows followed his aide to the lift which took them to the top floor.

"As you'll be flying out tonight Senator, we've put him in the presidential suite under an assumed name," Anthony informed him.

For the first time in a while Milo M Meadows III had an anxious feeling in the pit of his stomach, the feeling he would get when summoned to a meeting with Milo M Meadows II to be questioned over some perceived shortcoming. Even though he had become his father and according to many now exceeded the dead man in menace, the memory disturbed him.

Anthony knocked on the door and they waited. This was all wrong, Milo thought. The man should have been coming to him.

The door opened as far as the chain would let it.

CHAPTER 15

"Senator Meadows," Anthony announced and the door swung wide. An ordinary looking man stood there in a neat grey suit, white shirt and tie, a little smaller than average perhaps but fit and with eyes used to assessing danger or advantage in the seconds that could separate life from death in his line of work.

"Senator," Anthony said, "can I introduce you to Pietro LaBoucher."

The two men shook hands with the enthusiasm of two boxers about to enter the ring.

"Will you be wanting to return to the banqueting hall?" Anthony asked.

"No, I think we're done there."

"Well call me when you are through here Senator and I'll have the car take us to Hawkins Field. The pilot is keen to get away," the senator's aide said, "apparently some bad weather's coming in."

With the aide gone the two men found themselves alone together like two birds of prey thrown together by a storm.

"Bourbon, Senator?" LaBoucher eventually asked.

"Why not, as I'm paying for it."

"Ice?"

"Please."

The gangster poured the liquor and added the ice, passing one of the two glasses to the politician. They both sat down and studied one another.

"So what can I help you with Senator," LaBoucher asked at length.

"I've heard that you are working for Attorney General Stone."

"I never discuss my clients," LaBoucher told him with the probity of the professional he was.

"Well be that as it may," the Senator responded with barely disguised irritation. "I want you to do something for me."

"Could you be more specific?"

"I am assuming the public anger being directed against physicists and some other ungodly bastions of learning is being given a helping hand."

"I'm listening Senator."

"Supposing these activities were widened to include government, at first local and just here and there, but eventually national?"

"I imagine that would be expensive Senator."

"What about the national interest?"

CHAPTER 15

"I am of course a patriot," the gangster answered. "This fine country has given me a great deal, but it is a capitalist country."

"It is also a country bound by law."

"Laws which you make," the gangster pointed out.

"Can we stop beating about the bush?" The Senator was used to being obeyed, not played with. "Will you help me or not?"

Pietro had been doing some calculating in his head.

"What the hell's this?" Milo Meadows protested when he had taken in what was written on the piece of paper the gangster handed him. "This is robbery!"

Pietro shrugged and said nothing.

Senator Meadows pulled out his phone and called his aide.

"Anthony, come and get me. I'm done here."

The Senator sat in silence glowering as he weighed his options.

"Where to?" he asked eventually.

Pietro handed over another scrap of paper.

At the knock on the door candidate Meadows leapt up like a horse ready to bolt.

"I hope you beat that storm, Senator," the gangster called out after the departing politician from whom even feigned good manners had been squeezed by the humiliation of being outsmarted by a Frenchified Wop.

CHAPTER 15

16

AT the time Jay Chandler couldn't believe his luck. Ousting an incumbent was hard at the best of times. Besting a dead one could sometimes be harder. But the sympathy vote garnered by the Rationalist candidate selected to stand in Herbert Hollingsworth's place had not been enough. While Jay's was a fresh face it had become known in the weeks running up to the vote and even without a wife standing by his side, as voters generally expected, he'd won. 'Get a wife', Marjory Anhauser had advised when he announced his candidacy but in spite of some serious interest from Geraldine, a Dole Foods heiress he'd known since childhood, he'd held back.

On election night, surrounded by his team and buoyed

up by the growing realization that he was going to win, the consequences hadn't occurred to him. But on the way home after the celebrations as dawn punctured the San Francisco night wiping the blackboard clean he'd felt utterly alone. The lifeless buildings and empty streets tumbling down in the half-light to the black water of the bay seemed wholly devoid of any human presence. How could a city of almost a million people feel like a distant galactic outpost? 'Congressman Chandler.' He repeated it to himself several times, but it didn't help. At an intersection a cab crossed over with revellers in the back heading to - it didn't much matter where: doubtless to each other. An early gull swooped past and he envied the bird simply because it was alive and seemed to know what it was doing. For months every scrap of him had been focused on one thing: winning. Now he had and was consumed by an overwhelming sense of nothingness.

He tapped his phone and let it ring and ring and ring. A disoriented voice eventually answered. "Yes?" "Geri, it's Jay. Can I come round?"

He wasn't far from her block and she let him into the building. When the lift door opened she was standing waiting at her apartment door in a white nightdress, still sleepy under tousled hair.

"So you won – congratulations!" she said closing the door behind him. "Can I make you some coffee?"

"No."

She could see that he was utterly exhausted. Even that simple word had been forced out.

CHAPTER 16

Geri's housemate appeared, scowling at the commotion.

"What's going on?"

"It's only Jay, Jay Chandler," Geri explained.

"He's just been elected to Congress."

"Oh," responded the housemate and turned back into her room.

"Can I hold you?" Jay asked.

"Of course you can."

Geri stood there unsure how to respond, with the Congressman collapsed onto her like a windless sail. She could feel her own heart beating and wondered if his heart was beating at all. He smelt of smoke, alcohol and sweat but it wasn't unpleasant.

"Here, let's get you into bed," she said marveling at the boldness of her invitation. Here was a man she had known socially all her life, a man she liked, a man she thought she could like much more being ushered into her girly room and deposited onto her six foot by three foot bed. He fell face down onto it, his head burrowed deep into her pillow knocking Arthur, her old teddy bear, to one side. 'Poor Arthur' she said placing the bear onto a nearby shelf. 'Now don't look like that,' she rebuked. But the stuffed animal's black beady eyes just stared back.

She wondered if she should remove some of the new

Congressman's clothes. She took off his shoes and left it at that, but even this simple act gave her pleasure. She stared at him for a while before collecting clothes from a cupboard and withdrawing to the living room. Her bedside clock had almost reached six. So there was an hour to fill before she could leave for work and by the look of him the day would be half over before he stirred. She wrote a note and left it on the table – 'Jay. Help yourself to what you want and make sure the door is fully closed when you leave. Geri.' - and then stretched out on the couch, thinking.

* * *

It was well after midday before Jay managed to pull himself together. He read Geri's note, made himself some coffee and toast and then checked his phone: there were messages and missed calls galore. The sun was streaming in through the window and he felt on top of the world. The night before seemed to stop in his mind at his victory speech and the hours afterward had dissipated into oblivion. He couldn't exactly remember how or why he'd ended up in Geri's apartment, but it didn't seem odd. He'd collected her so many times for functions they'd both gone to. She hadn't been at his campaign headquarters although he had thought of asking her.

An hour must have passed before he'd dealt with family and other well-wishers. The political professionals anxious to ride on his coat tails he could handle later. The last of the 'good calls' he wanted to reply to was from Carrie Holden. They hadn't spoken in a while. Her message was simple: "Well done. You had at least one physicist in your corner!" He called back.

"Carrie?"

CHAPTER 16

"Yes."

"It's Jay. Thank you for your message."

"So you are now an official persecutor of my profession!" she laughed.

"Just of its sweeping assumptions," he answered a little guiltily.

"Well someone has to get us out of this mess, so it might as well be you," she fired back.

"The Nationalists did pretty well too," he told her, "and their way of seeing the world is very different from the way we Moralists see it. The Rationalists are still comatose."

"Scary!"

"Yes. But the limbo we are currently in is almost the worst of all worlds. With the Rationalists sitting on their butts waiting for a free market miracle, the President's hands are tied. The Nationalists want him out and we just aren't strong enough to help him. I think the growing chaos is playing more into their hands than into ours."

"Surely people know where that will lead."

"Right now I'm not sure they care. They just want this nightmare to end. Anyway, enough gloom. What is my favorite physicist doing? Have you taken up that position at Mauna Kea?"

Carrie laughed. "Not exactly!"

"So what are you doing?"

"I'm working at Walmart here in Gilroy."

"Walmart! Jesus Carrie, what happened?"

"Ever since the Centre for Applied Physics was closed down John Franks, my supervisor, has become as invisible as dark matter. Without his signature the university won't award me the degree and without the degree I can't take up the posting. I am feeling a bit like John Yossarian in *Catch 22*."

"Hell Carrie, I am sorry. That's terrible." As a freshly minted congressman for the Moralist Party, Jay was beginning to feel accountable.

"I don't suppose you're personally to blame Jay, but physicists are being given a pretty good beating right now. As the most rational of Rationalists I suppose we had it coming, but not all of us are as arrogant as we are being portrayed."

"No doubt," Jay conceded. "But when scientists peddle books with mocking titles like *The God Delusion* you can see why that view persists."

"Look Jay, I've got to go now. My break's come to an end. Just sort things out!"

"I'll do my best," he assured her, with little conviction. "I'll call you when I'm next at the ranch."

CHAPTER 16

"You do that."

* * *

Marjory Anhauser threw a party for her new protégé. She had no time for the view that celebrating while half her countrymen suffered might be insensitive. A win was a win and should be properly marked. The Chronicle was there in force along with a whole host of social worthies and political operators, some renounced Rationalists several of whom had simply tossed a coin as their way of choosing between the alternatives. Their hostess was known to be more generous than Milo M Meadows III which doubtless drew a number to the cause and of course there were likely to be one or two invisible ones who continued to flirt with all three parties for as long as they could get away with it. This was politics after all and politics was a reflection of the human soul.

Dean Jimbalaya had scurried across from his reconfigured ivory tower in the East – "I wouldn't miss one of your celebrations for the world, Marjory," he had preened. Unwisely adding the gush: "The Marjory Anhauser Theological Institute owes you everything," which had evoked her corrective "and you think I don't know that Dean?," a put-down he barely noticed being the consummate academic survivor that he was. The Reverend Richard Preston had sent his apologies.

Marjory, standing in front of the large cathedral window of her living room which framed the bay and the now floodlit Golden Gate Bridge beyond tapped the microphone. The chatter subsided and the servers with the canapés retreated into the kitchen.

CHAPTER 16

"A warm welcome to you all," she began. "I will keep my remarks brief because we are here for our new congressman, Jay Chandler, whose impressive victory for the Moralist cause we celebrate.

"As Moralists we have one goal: to change the context within which our decisions are made. Some physicists – and yes we can talk about them even in polite company [laughter] – some physicists," she repeated, "believe that the geometry of the dimensions that underpin our universe determine its character. Different geometries produce different universes. Well strange as it may seem that is exactly what we believe. Change the moral context and life will evolve in a different way.

"Science breaks things down into bits and is passive – it seeks to find out how things work. Morality attempts to put things back together again and is active. It seeks to tell us how things should work.

"For the best part of two millennia the great religions attempted to provide a moral context for human action. Unfortunately form came to take precedence over substance and it was this form that scientific enquiry blew apart.

"But we are coming to realize that knowledge on its own is meaningless. Knowing that this causes that might give us the illusion of control, but it is not control. Governments are good at counting things – well quite good [some more laughter], but are much less good at solving problems. Rationalists, I think, have been affected by the fatalism of the scientists who say that mankind is a fluke and that life as we know it must end. So let things run as they will, Rationalists are inclined to say –

CHAPTER 16

because they will anyway.

"We Moralists think differently. For us the present is everything and each day that passes during which we fail to nurture and enhance life as a whole is a day lost. For us this is the deep truth that lies at the heart of everything, a truth some of us like to call God.

"Now that is quite enough from me," she concluded. "So Jay, perhaps you would like to come up and say a few words." Her tone was more of command than request.

As Marjory Anhauser stepped aside, the gathering, visibly moved and not a little surprised that their hostess had a brain as well as a fortune, a possibility that had not occurred to all of them, clapped respectfully and Jay made his way to the front.

The new congressman thanked their hostess, his benefactor; he thanked his other supporters and he thanked the Chronicle. He then went on to explain the importance of the President's Home Stabilization Initiative outlining how it would help to get the economy going again and rebuild communities. He described how the Rationalists were still sitting on the fence hoping that things would turn around of their own volition as their economic theories suggested they eventually would, and failing that were waiting to see whether they needed to jump toward the Nationalists or Moralists in order to maintain their hold on power. The contempt he felt for these parties was palpable and spread around the room as he hoped it would, earning Marjory's applause as he stepped from behind the microphone back into the throng of well-wishers, many eager to shake his hand.

CHAPTER 16

"Nicely done Jay," she said as he passed her, adding approvingly in a louder voice than he would have liked: "I see you have brought Geraldine Cooke with you: excellent!"

Paul Proctor, The Chronicle's religion editor was one of the first to pigeonhole him and push for an interview. "Was the nature of religion changing," he wondered, suggesting that perhaps they could discuss that. Lesley Sharp followed, keen that Jay outline how the President's initiative would be funded, something she said The Chronicle's readers were anxious to know. He had often wondered how himself but said he would be happy to meet with her although avoided being pinned down to a time. 'Call my office' was a political tactic easily learned.

Hildegard Prentice, a 14th District resident and generous contributor drew his attention to a damaged fire hydrant on the corner of Hickey and Catalina and her neighbor Goram LaGuardia complained that little Imperial Park was swarming, as he put it, with rough sleepers – "don't get me wrong Congressman: I have great sympathy for these unfortunates, but Imperial's not the right park for them." Jay pointed out that these were really matters for the Mayor of Pacifica, but he'd do what he could.

Seeing that her guest of honor was cornered, Marjory Anhauser swept up to rescue him.

"Now Hildi and you too Gor, let my congressman circulate. There's someone I want him to meet."

Jay found himself being guided by the arm toward a humpty dumpty shaped man holding forth in front of a small circle of guests who seemed to be hanging on his every word.

CHAPTER 16

"Dean, I'd like you to meet our new congressman," she said, parting his circle like the waters of the Red Sea.

"Dean Jimbalaya has just been telling us about the Multiverse Marjory," enthused one of his star-struck admirers, an announcement that made even the Dean blush as the subject was tantamount to discussing the joys of oral sex at a prayer meeting.

While Marjory scattered the Dean's little coterie, Jay remembered that he had told her about his friend's academic impasse. She had not forgotten.

"Congratulations Congressman. A fine victory," the Dean enthused as Marjory left them to it.

Jay thanked him but doubted if a man from the East Coast had any knowledge whatsoever of San Francisco's 14th District.

"Now Dean, I believe you know a friend of mine, Carrie Holden, whose doctoral supervisor seems to have gone missing."

The Dean looked puzzled for a moment as the name Carrie Holden clearly did not resonate.

"The astrophysicist," Jay prompted. "I think she said John Franks was the name of her supervisor."

"Ah yes, Carrie Holden. Such a bright young lady," he conjured up. "I have all her papers just waiting for Professor Franks's signature."

"If this Professor Franks has disappeared, can't you just wave that requirement?" Jay asked.

"I wish I could," he said with what looked like a hint of real sympathy. "But he is the one who knows her work and following the .. er .. changes I don't have any physicist left who could attest to it."

"Well, for heavens sake, someone must know where he is, surely?"

The Dean appeared uncomfortable and looked around to make sure that no one was paying attention to their conversation.

"You are in Washington now, right?" he ventured.

"Well I haven't actually taken up my position yet," Jay admitted.

"When you do, try Senator Grasser's office."

"Senator Grasser: the Chairman of the Senate Armed Services Committee?"

"Yes, but please don't mention my name," the Dean urged.

"What do I say when I get there?" Jay asked.

"Say you are interested in Alpha-Omega."

"That sounds Biblical."

"You could say that," the Dean agreed with a distinctly

sickly smile. "Now I have already said too much."

Once again, like the all-seeing conductor she was, Marjory Anhauser approached, this time with Geraldine Cooke on her arm.

"Now Jay," she scolded, "you are neglecting your young lady."

From then on she had them circulating like the couple she thought they should be.

By half seven most guests had left and Marjory agreed that he should leave with his date for the dinner he had booked at Quince. While he waited to collect his coat and for Geri to get herself ready Jay found himself standing next to Mark Stetz, the Chronicle's social editor who as usual was keeping his hand on society's pulse. Mark had interviewed him for a subtle 'puff piece' at the start of his campaign.

"I believe I owe you," Jay said thinking of the glowing article and unaware that Herbert Hollingsworth had fallen foul of the journalist's darker craft.

"Not at all: you were the better candidate," Mark replied.

"It was a heart attack apparently, that did for my opponent."

"Yes, apparently so," Mark confirmed. "Overwork no doubt. Try not to go the same way."

Geri appeared from the powder room smelling delicious

CHAPTER 16

and looking divine. The Chronicle's social editor smiled and wished them both a good evening. There were some things people just didn't need to know.

CHAPTER 16

17

IMPERIAL was a pretty little park, although certainly not one of the most notable, but he thought he should have a look even if only to tell Mr. LaGuardia that he had. As he approached he realized that in his short political career he had not once visited any of the encampments for the dispossessed that had sprung up in parks around the country. His campaign manager had advised him not to bother as, according to him, there were no votes in it. Keeping the homeless off the golf courses seemed to be a greater priority.

He stopped in Imperial Drive and walked through. What he found was no longer a recreational area but a town within a town more like a Middle Eastern refugee camp. Tents of all shapes and sizes filled the small plateau, laid out in a sort of order suggesting that this had become an organized community. Children played in the sun and a few adults went about their business, whatever that business was. The surrounding houses were not grand but neat, save for those with *For Sale* signs which were starting to look tired and overgrown. He wondered if their past owners had just move across into the park.

"Can I help you?"

The question caught him unprepared. He had been staring at the unexpected scene, taking it all in and trying to make sense of it.

"Sorry?" Jay said unsure that he had heard correctly.

"I'm Peter. I guess you could say that I'm in charge around here."

"In the camp?

"Yes, in the camp. It sort of just happened initially, but we now have elections and I was elected."

"So was I," replied Jay.

"Oh," responded Peter concerned that there might have been a coup behind his back. "What of?"

"Here; the 14th District – for Congress," Jay told him.

"I see," acknowledged Peter with relief more than interest.

CHAPTER 17

"To be honest none of that registers much around here."

"How many people are living in the camp?" Jay asked.

"Around 200," Peter replied. "This is one of the smaller camps which makes it better than others in the city. There are sixty families which is manageable. We have a school, a store and even a tiny clinic: all run by volunteers from the camp."

"What's wrong with the state school?" Jay asked. "Sunset Ridge Elementary is just down the hill, isn't it?"

"Sure. But funding's tight and they've cut right back. Here money isn't an issue. We have two or three teachers in the camp with time to give."

"And the store?"

"Oh that doesn't take money either. But if you want something you have to bring something. That's how it works."

"And these 'somethings'; where do people get them?" Jay wondered.

"During the day people go searching for anything that could be useful. Even in these hard times you'd be surprised at how much is thrown out. The big supermarkets are a great source. Anything out of date we'll usually snap up."

"Are the churches involved at all?"

"The Westside Baptist and the Filipino Seventh-Day

Adventist have been pretty helpful, as has The Church of the Good Shepherd," Peter told him. "All three have parishioners in the camp."

"Is crime a problem?" Jay asked him.

"No, not in the camp. But we have had on-going issues with what goes on in the woods down below."

"What sort of issues?"

"Well let's say there are boys and girls, men and women, making a living down there in ways that don't sit too well with our family orientation," Peter explained. "We tried to persuade them to join us and one or two seemed interested but that wasn't what their leaders wanted."

"'Their leaders' – how do you mean?"

"There's a large camp in the hills at the back of Fairway Park south of here run on very different lines to us. I'd say it was run by the Mob frankly, but that's not how those down below see it. They think we're plain stupid when there is good money to be made selling things to the affluent which the affluent can't get legally."

"Sex and drugs?"

"Of course, sex and drugs - isn't it always? - Those things that relieve the monotony of empty lives and destabilize normal ones. There were some ugly moments between us at first, but now we leave each other alone. I think your predecessor enjoyed the dark side, so if that's what you're after you need to come in off Horizon Way."

"No it's not," snapped Jay offended that his noble intentions might have been misconstrued and that the name of his dead opponent could be so casually blackened. "I just came to see for myself what went on here and to respond to a resident who would like to see this camp moved."

"Moved to where?" laughed Peter. "I expect your complainant was Goram LaGuardia. He has been to see me several times. And you know the funny thing is he's never complained about what goes on down the hill."

"I imagine he doesn't know about it," huffed Jay, still smarting from Peter's earlier suggestion.

"Right!"

The two stood in silence watching the comings and goings in front of them, one with a degree of satisfaction that he had had a hand in recreating the semblance of civil society, the other with a degree of incomprehension that a parallel world should exist over which his new writ simply did not run.

"What do you make of the President's Home Stabilization Initiative?" he asked eventually.

"Oh, I am afraid we've given up listening to the promises of politicians," Peter laughed. "What is his initiative?"

"It's a way of helping people get back into their homes." Jay explained.

"What, helping them get back into the system that spat them out in the first place?" Peter responded. "I don't think so! That'll be a mighty tough sell, if you ask me."

Just then a good-looking woman approached with a young girl in tow who Peter gathered up onto his shoulders.

"Look I must get on," he said. "But please come back. And while you are here why don't you look around. You won't be eaten," adding with a wry laugh, "at least you won't be so long as you don't tell anyone that you are part of our great government!"

Jay did walk around and was impressed by the neatness and purposefulness of the place. On a sun-filled day there was always the outside, but in the rain and the fog being stuck inside a tent would have been less appealing. He remembered his own camping days during which discomfort was easily borne by the knowledge that one would be home eventually. For his nation's first settlers there had been no turning back and their early years had been far from idyllic. But as he walked back to the car three things occurred to him. The first was that community life and economic freedom were not always compatible. The second was that the gap between individuals and their government might have become unbridgeable. The third thing to strike him was that while people would come together naturally, they still needed a 'Peter' to guide them – for good or ill.

* * *

CHAPTER 17

Imperial Park was in Pacifica and Pacifica was in his District, so Congressman Chandler decided he would show his face at City Hall. The Spanish had been the first to explore the coast which until then had been the exclusive preserve of the Ohlone Indians. The coastline was so shrouded in fog that the Spaniards had missed the San Francisco Bay until Gaspar de Portolà y Rovira anchored where Pacifica now is in 1769 and climbed the ridge behind it. In the distance he could see the inlet, a perfectly protected anchorage. Seven years later his king established the Presidio de San Francisco.

In 1821 New Spain, as it had come to be called, broke free from its European parent becoming Mexico but following defeat in the Mexican-American war, the land was ceded to the young, thrusting United States. That had taken place in 1847. Latinos had not given up, however, and Spanish was now recognized as California's second language, although in Pacifica those of Asian origin had just pulled ahead leaving those describing themselves as white with only a slender majority. Jay paid attention to these things, or at least his aides did: people had become 'types' first and human beings a distant second, which he rather idly thought could have had some bearing on his nation's problems.

He crossed over Highway 1, the coast road from Los Angeles four hundred miles away, with a clear view of the Pacific and the municipal pier jutting into it like a weak pencil mark, and turned up Santa Monica Avenue. City Hall was not impressive, but with two stories was higher than many of the houses nearby. Its clean, simple lines seemed appropriate for a municipality of just 37,000, although a fresh coat of paint was overdue, doubtless reflecting hard times.

CHAPTER 17

A sign in reception above a bell said please ring which he did but no one came. The building appeared to have been deserted.

So he started to wander around, peering into the rooms on the ground floor and finding papers strewn on desks as if an alarm had sent their organizers scurrying away for safety. "Hello!" he called out intermittently in case he was caught and thought to be a wrong-doer.

In a back room with three untidy desks he came across a light blue budgerigar in a cage. The bird was singing away and fluttering between two slender poles that straddled the inside of its domain. Its 'feeder' had seed in it and there was water so the little creature was being cared for and seemed happy enough. Two cactus pots sat on a window ledge. Outside the window several sparrows were frisking an oleander bush for insects free to come and go as they pleased.

Discovering no one downstairs he thought he might as well try up but only found more empty rooms. Peering into one, however, he came upon a somewhat disheveled middle-aged man in shirt sleeves wearing spectacles staring intently at a screen and guiding a computer mouse with one hand while his other tapped furiously away at a calculator on the desk. Startled the man looked up, his tone sharp born out of surprise.

"Yes?"

"I am sorry," Jay apologized. "But I couldn't find anyone."

"They are all at Raymond's."

CHAPTER 17

"You're the only one here?"

"I don't like Chinese."

"I see," said Jay, although he didn't, but thought he would introduce himself anyway. "I'm Congressman Chandler. I was in the area and decided to make a courtesy call, but I have clearly come at a bad time."

"Not Hollingsworth?" the man said, struggling to get his bearings.

"No. Hollingsworth lost. I'm Chandler."

The man stared back for a moment trying to clear his head of the numbers that had been swimming around inside it like an unruly shoal of mackerel.

"Hardly surprising. He didn't do much. I'm the accountant round here, by the way: Don Festin.

Ray stepped forward and shook the clammy hand offered him.

"I don't imagine things are very easy at the moment," he said.

Don Festin's laugh was a mixture of the desperate and the lunatic.

"Well where do you want me to start?" he began. "Our budget is a mess. At the end of last year it was awful and we thought we had a fix on things but this year it is even worse and next year promises to be worse still. Thirty percent of our revenue comes from property taxes and this has collapsed. Upwards of fourteen percent of our homes are for sale and that is just the tip of the iceberg. Another ten percent are not making their payments and there is little point in forcing them from their homes when their homes are not going to sell anyway. Trade is way down across the board so the sales tax is bringing in less and transfers from the state have been reduced as well. We've cut everything we can cut and some of our staff are even working on a volunteer basis. That's what the meeting at Raymond's is about: who is willing to work for less and who can work for nothing. I just don't know what to do, frankly. I can't make the numbers work."

Jay felt like someone visiting a patient in hospital with terminal cancer, at a loss for words.

"Whose is the budgerigar downstairs?" he asked.

"That's Mary's. She'd sooner not eat than let that bird starve," he said.

"Luckily birds don't each much."

"That's true," agreed Don Festin, as happy as Jay not to focus for a moment on the train wreck unfolding around him which he was powerless to do anything about.

"I don't suppose the Federal Government could step in?" he asked the congressman in a tone of such sorry resignation that it neither would nor could that

CHAPTER 17

the question almost devoured itself.

"There is the President's Home Stabilization Initiative, if he could only get it past the Rationalists in congress," Jay proffered, now knowing that what Pacifica's accountant needed was an immediate miracle.

"You're with the Moralists then?

"Yes," Jay admitted.

"I'm inclined to the Nationalists, myself," retorted Don. "They may not be very nice people, but I think they'll get things done."

Jay asked him to keep an open mind, thanked him for his time and left. This had not turned out to be the triumphal visit to one of his outposts that he had imagined. He hadn't even mentioned the encampment in Imperial Park which was beginning to look like a place that made sense. As he drove away he passed another: *Raymond's Excellent Chinese Cuisine* was busy, doubtless easing its customers' sorrows.

CHAPTER 17

CHAPTER 17

18

IT began as a stunt. Two students from Messiah College, Mechanicsburg, Pennsylvania – Matthew Fenton and Robert Hardy set out to 'capture' Professor Olsen who was to give a lecture at Penn State's Center for Gravitational Wave Physics on the subject of Dark Matter which the two students thought sounded suitably satanic. The idea had been brought to them by a third student from Penn State itself, Saskia Brown. The trio's plan was to waylay the scientist before the talk in order to prevent it from taking place and then generate as much publicity as possible out of the furor. As an outspoken atheist the Messiah students regarded Professor Olsen as a good example of the godless world they sought to overthrow.

However their exploit went wrong at its outset. An hour before the lecture was due to be given and as agreed, they arrived at the hotel where Professor Olsen was staying pretending to be the drivers slated to take him to the auditorium. As the plan's organizer from the Penn State end, Saskia went in to collect the academic.

While Matt and Rob waited nervously in the car they started to express doubts about the wisdom of their scheme although hesitantly at first as neither wanted to be the first to reveal his feelings. But just as they were about to discuss how best to abandon the abduction altogether, Saskia appeared and guided her charge into the back seat next to Rob before climbing into the front beside Matt.

"Drive," she said curtly. "I'll give you directions."

As the two young men looked at one another in the rear view mirror, the feeling of disorientation and panic they felt was total. The Professor Olsen sitting in the back of their car was not the Professor Olsen they had expected.

"You are Professor Olsen?" Matt asked as casually as he could while trying to make eye contact with his passenger in the mirror as the car sped along.

"Yes, Professor Freja Olsen from Denmark," she answered, looking up briefly from the text of her presentation.

If he had ever wondered what blood turning cold felt like he now knew.

CHAPTER 18

"Right here," Saskia instructed in a calm but firm voice.

They appeared to be traveling away from the center down East College Avenue. The Penn State woman made a quick call: "We're ten minutes away," was all she said. Freja Olsen was so engrossed in her notes illuminated by the light of her mobile phone, that she was oblivious to the tension inside the car or to its direction.

On Saskia's order Matt turned into Puddintown Lane passing a sign to the Millbroke Nature Center.

"Pull in here," she told him.

The car stopped next to a metal storage unit, grey painted with only the number 1034 to identify it. Matt looked at Saskia but she was already getting out and moving to the passenger door which she opened, skillfully taking the mobile phone from their startled guest.

"OK Professor," she announced. "It's time to get out."

Until that moment Freja Olsen had suspected nothing, so absorbed had she been in the talk she was about to give. But now she looked terrified as two men appeared out of the shadows. Saskia nodded and one reached in and began to drag her from the car as she resisted, shouting.

"What the hell is going on? What are you doing? I am a Danish citizen!"

Aghast Matt and Rob watched her being led away into

the darkness struggling, her mouth now taped. It had all taken less than a minute.

"Carry this with you back to Messiah," Saskia instructed handing Rob their captive's mobile phone, "and then destroy it."

"Aren't you coming with us?" Matt asked plaintively.

The Penn State woman gave him a withering look and then she too disappeared into the trees.

The two friends sat in silence, their senses shredded by what they had just witnessed.

"Fucking hell," Rob exhaled eventually. "That was awful!"

But his friend was still speechless so he kept talking.

"Have you any idea where we are?"

The car was parked in open ground off a back road with a busy overpass a hundred yards ahead. Matt studied the position finder on his mobile phone.

"I guess that's the Mount Nittany Expressway," he announced after a while, relieved to have had something tangible to concentrate on.

"Well if it'll take us back to Mechanicsburg," Rob urged, "let's bloody well take it!"

Naturally it was not that easy. They had to backtrack down

CHAPTER 18

Puddintown to East College before they could get onto it. But eventually they did and drove south, in silence. It wasn't until they had crossed the Susquehanna River for the first time, with its headwaters in New York State that they felt able to say anything and even then it didn't amount to much. Rob, now sitting in front alongside Matt, was the first to try.

"What are we going to do?" he asked, as much to himself as to Matt.

"Get rid of this damn phone," was the best his friend could come up with.

And so as they crossed the Susquehanna for the second time Matt threw it out of the window.

* * *

President Dukes was incandescent. It was all over the papers: "Danish professor abducted!" "Famous young scientist snatched!" The Nationalist Clarion screamed: "*Is anyone safe?*" Knocking self-satisfied physicists off their priestly perch was one thing, but spiriting one away in full view – a young female and foreign guest to boot – well that just didn't play well. What made it even worse was that rumors were circulating that her abductors were from a Christian college. And if all that was not bad enough, an interview with the woman's distraught mother had just been published stating that Freja Olsen was a regular churchgoer. Angry at being left out of the limelight, the renowned evolutionary biologist Professor Karl Olsen was claiming that he had been the real target, declaring that what he called 'the God crowd' had clearly fallen short when it came to divine guidance.

CHAPTER 18

"So what the hell do we know, Seymour?" the President asked his Attorney General.

"I think it's what we don't know that's important here, Mr. President."

"Please Seymour, no riddles!"

"Well all we do know is that an hour before she was due to present a paper at the Center for Gravitational Physics at Penn State University Professor Freja Olsen was accompanied out of her hotel by a young female."

"Is that it?"

"No not quite. When she left her hotel Professor Olsen was carrying her mobile phone and it was switched on. Now as you know, the Europeans are more attuned to data privacy than we are, but according to the Danish police the tracking record suggests that the Professor was driven to the Mount Nittany Expressway, although not directly. It looks as though her driver took a wrong turn and had to double back before reaching it. The signal then went dead near Harrisburg. Our guess is that either the device was destroyed there, suggesting that was the end of the journey, or it was thrown into the Susquehanna River while the car it was in drove on."

"Well that's quite a bit that we know," encouraged the President.

"Yes, quite a bit that we know about the young lady's mobile phone," countered Seymour Stone.

CHAPTER 18

"Go on."

"I have been doing some digging and it so happens that there is a large itinerant camp north east of the Penn State campus more or less exactly where the car carrying Freja Olsen doubled back."

"Are you suggesting she might have left the car there?"

"It's a possibility."

"Is she an activist?"

"Not as far as we know."

"So if she did leave the car," the President asked, "why would she leave behind her mobile phone?"

"Perhaps she was forced to," Mr. President.

Henry Dukes drummed the desk top with his fingers. He felt so boxed in. Perhaps Milo Meadows was right. There were times when a president needed to act and not be tied down by Congressional pigmies like Gulliver was in Lilliput.

"And why was the phone left on?" he continued.

"That's precisely the question," encouraged the Attorney General like a school master whose pupil was on the verge of grasping the essential point.

"So you think she might have been abducted and her

mobile phone left on to throw us off the scent?"

"It's a possibility," confirmed Attorney Stone. "And there may be more. Her phone went dead about fourteen miles from Messiah, the college her abductors are rumored to have come from, which raises the question, where did those rumors originate?"

"The Nationalists?"

Seymour shrugged.

"What is the FBI saying?" the President asked.

"That's another issue, Mr. President. The Nationalists have long tentacles. The FBI is telling me they have nothing. Until this impasse between Nationalists, Rationalists and Moralists is resolved I fear the machinery of government will keep clogging."

"Another one for Senator Meadows," Henry Dukes mumbled.

"Sorry?"

"Oh nothing," he answered with a sigh. "So what do you propose?"

"Assuming the patsies in all of this are in Messiah, we need to find them."

"And find the woman," added the President.

CHAPTER 18

"If she's alive," cautioned his Attorney.

"Jesus, Seymour: that's all we need!"

* * *

Three weeks after the abduction, with the event gaining ever more coverage in the media as a distraction from the nation's ills, Matthew Fenton and Robert Hardy, who had both set out to be good Christians, could bear their guilt no more and confessed the whole grisly business to their college principal. He called his old friend Richard Preston who called the President. There were, the Reverend indicated, two young men who wished to talk but with a skeptical view of White House security which upset the President – "Jesus Pastor, I am supposed to be the most powerful man in the world!" - he refused to give any more details over the telephone.

It didn't take Stone long to work out that these were the Messiah students he was searching for and so he flew down to meet them. Their hapless tale supported his worst fears. A quick call confirmed them: there was no student called Saskia Brown at Penn State. This had been a skillfully planned operation to discredit the Moralists. The key question now was who was behind it. If it was LaBoucher he'd want to sell his captive to the highest bidder. But if it was some renegade Nationalists who had already been paid to make the Moralists look bad, the woman would most likely be dead in a ditch by now with her throat cut.

Seymour told his president that he was following up on some useful leads and left it at that. The Messiah principal was only too happy to keep the whole matter buried from view. Far less happy were the two students whose confession had not brought them absolution.

CHAPTER 18

19

Jay found the office allocated to him inside the Rayburn Building on Capitol Hill. He felt excited as well as completely lost. How on earth did anyone actually achieve anything?

He remembered a mind game one of his teachers had made his pupils play. 'Now I want you all to close your eyes and imagine yourselves flying out of the window, can you do that?' The boys and girls would screw their eyes tight shut and launch themselves like Peter Pan out of the window and across the school playing fields into the trees beyond. 'Hands up everyone who managed it,' the teacher would then ask. A forest of eager little hands would spring up. 'Very good,' he would congratulate. 'Now,' he instructed 'I want you to take that journey for real.'

Puzzlement would abound and a sea of disappointed faces stare back. 'You see, my young friends,' he would then tell them, 'it is far easier to imagine doing something than it is to actually do it.'

After the disillusionment had started to fade he would continue. 'The reason for this,' he would tell them, 'is because of something called reality and why we need to understand it.' At which point some precocious child was sure to announce: 'but Sir, if I had a plane…' which would allow the teacher to complete his lesson.

'Excellent point Wendy, or Peter or whoever the little genius was. And how long did it take mankind to develop the airplane?' 'A very long time, Sir,' would come back the enthusiastic reply. 'So there you have it,' he would conclude. 'It is only when we combine our understanding of reality with our imagination that we can do really wonderful things.' Or as Jay was coming to understand, in the absence of morality do some truly barbarous things as well.

He had almost appointed all of the 18 staff he was allowed, split between his District and DC offices. At first he was surprised at the number but quickly realized that dealing with the executive branch, congressional committees, lobbyists and the demands of those he was there to represent could occupy a small army if he let them. He'd appointed Larry Allen, an old school friend who'd worked in DC for several years, as his chief of staff.

Correspondence was well filtered before it reached his desk but a hand written note attached to an almost completed form had got through. 'Just Professor John Franks's signature needed', the note read. He quickly realized that it was the document that

CHAPTER 19

stood between Carrie Holden and her degree. Whether he had pricked Dean Jimbalaya's conscience, or as he thought more likely, secured his interest as one of Marjory Anhauser's blue-eyed boys, Carrie's future had found its way into his hands.

"Someone from our District?" asked Larry who intended to make it his business to keep a close eye on anything that hit the congressman's desk.

"No, a friend."

There was a fine line between discretion and being on top of things and one of a staffer's great joys lay in being as close to his politician as was possible without sleeping with him, which of course some did, generally to everyone's detriment.

"Does Alpha-Omega mean anything to you?" Jay asked.

"No. Should it?"

"Do you know anyone in Senator Arlen Grasser's office?"

"Yes," Larry told him. "I do see a girl, Myra Lupton, from time to time at one of DC's watering holes where we staffers trade gossip: trying to get as much as we can from one another while giving as little as possible away. The senator's pretty big around here: not someone to mess with."

"Well, see what you can find out," Jay instructed.

* * *

CHAPTER 19

It was early evening and his staffers had gone home. Jay was at his desk beginning to think that he could see how things might work. His teacher's lesson about the difference between imagination and reality kept coming back to him. A nation was like the human body, the man had later said. What a society could imagine was a function of its ability to conjure up scenarios from past experience. What it could do, however, was constrained by how it was structured.

It seemed to him that the analogy did not stop there. As with the body most of what went on was largely automatic and had developed to keep the system operating in a self-reinforcing way. Individual deviations from the established pattern would quickly wither unless they brought back some benefit to the whole, just as happens when bees discover a new source of nectar and communicate this to the hive. If a searching bee got lost and died, he rather doubted if its compatriots would even notice. For a society to change not only required the recognition amongst a significant cohort that it was warranted, but a reconfiguration of the power relations that underpinned it, all of which might be beyond its ability. A given body allied to a given set of tools could only do so much.

At the moment the Rationalists were hoping that their tried and tested laissez-faire arrangements would right the ship in spite of mounting evidence to the contrary. In contrast, Moralists and Nationalists were arguing for intervention but of a very different kind. Nationalists wanted active intervention from the top to eliminate the symptoms of the malaise which they saw as its cause. Moralists sought to push power back down to individuals and their communities in order to reinvigorate a shared moral framework. Across government people who depended upon positions for their identity, not to mention their daily bread, waited for the fog of war between the factions to clear, even as countless little battles between opportunity and principle were being fought out.

As he sifted through the papers on his desk his thoughts traveled back to the encampment and Peter's remark about Herbert Hollingsworth. Had his opponent a hidden life that had somehow played into his defeat? He had heard a few rumors certainly, but then there were always rumors and people died of heart attacks all the time. He did regard the Chronicle's social editor as a dark horse and sensed that there was something he was not being told. His grandfather had once warned him that if he really was contemplating a life in politics he would need a thick skin and if not a devious character then certainly a devious mind.

R*I*N*G

The unwelcome sound from the telephone on his desk made him jump. Impatiently he reached across for the receiver.

"Yes?"

"Congressman Chandler?"

"Speaking."

"Congressman, this is Senator Arlen Grasser and I'm mighty glad to have caught you."

Jay all but sprang to attention from his chair at the sound of the senator's gravelly overture.

CHAPTER 19

"Good evening Senator."

"Now son, I'm not going to beat about the bush on this, but I hear you've been expressing an interest in Alpha-Omeega."

"Well Senator, I was....."

But the Senator had no need of his confirmation and issued a simple instruction instead.

"Be at Andrews Air Force Base tomorrow at six-thirty a.m. sharp. Have you got that son? Tell 'em you're flying out with Senator Grasser."

"Yes Sir, Senator."

"… and Congressman, if you were planning a dinner date tomorrow evening, best cancel. You won't be back till close on midnight."

With that the Senator rang off leaving Jay holding a purring piece of plastic and wondering what the hell had just happened. After he'd recovered his balance he sent a text message to Larry: 'don't know what you did but will be away all day with Arlen Grasser. Reschedule appointments.' It would be an early start, so time to go home. He felt energized. Things were happening. Note to self: 'must not forget to take Carrie's form.' Surely he was on the trail of her illusive John Franks.

* * *

It took him just over thirty minutes to reach Andrews, but

then there were the security checks and finding where to park so it was as well he'd given himself time. Not long after half six he'd been ushered through the complex and into the back of the waiting Gulfstream. The pilot and co-pilot were already in the cockpit and a flight attendant was busy in the galley. She'd smiled at him and shown him to his seat so he was expected. Shortly before seven a large man in his early seventies with thick white hair wearing a loose-fitting suit and tie boarded accompanied by two men in military uniforms along with a civilian with thick glasses who would not have stood out in any crowd. The attendant made a fuss of her VIPs and seated them at the front in a circular arrangement so they could talk. The steps were retracted and the plane was soon in the air traveling to he did not know where.

"Some breakfast Sir," asked the attendant who had introduced herself as Gena after she had lavished attention on the foursome in her charge, one of whom appeared to be an army Lieutenant General and another an air force Colonel. Jay was hungry and readily accepted her offer.

"Do you know where we are going?" he asked.

"West," she told him with an engaging smile.

It was clear he was not in the circle of trust although consoled himself with the fact that he was at least on the plane; but why? Senator Grasser was not known to be a chaser after young men or capricious so there will have been a reason. He thought it unlikely that the mere mention of Alpha-Omega, whatever that was, would have been enough to trigger such a reaction. No, the Senator was up to something and the young congressman from San Francisco's 14th District had become a pawn in his game.

They had been following the dawn for close to three hours. Gena, who was from Florida, had been happy to talk from time to time but had not thrown much light on their itinerary other than to confirm what he already knew: they were not expected to be back at Andrews until eleven that night. Jay was looking out of the window watching the land below gradually change from lush green to a patchwork of more arid brown when he realized the large man with the white hair was standing next to him.

"Glad you could make the flight, Congressman."

Senator Grasser's voice was unmistakable.

"Now son," his new companion began as he sat down beside him, "I want you to tell me about your interest in Alpha-Omeega."

Jay explained that he had no interest in Alpha-Omega other than it seemed to be associated with a Professor John Franks who had disappeared and whose signature was needed so that a friend could get her degree.

"Is this lady your sweetheart then Congressman?"

"We go back a long way Senator," Jay answered, unsure exactly what Carrie had become in his pantheon. "At the moment she is stuck working in Walmart."

"So what does the lady need this pro-fessa to sign?"

CHAPTER 19

Jay opened the satchel he had brought and showed the Senator Carrie's almost completed doctoral release papers. Arlen Grasser studied them intently.

"A most impressive young woman," he concluded. "It would be a mortal sin to have her languishing in that great emporium."

"I think so too Senator, even if her subject is not too popular right now."

"When a priesthood claims more than it can deliver, Congressman, the people's anger is fierce."

"It would certainly seem so," Jay agreed.

"Now if you would permit me," Senator Grasser said, still holding Carrie's documentation, "I just may be able to help. I'll get these back to you when we fly home this evening."

Jay agreed without hesitation and watched the Senator heave his great body onto an adjacent side sofa in the cabin and seemingly go to sleep with the satchel carrying Carrie's papers balanced on his heaving chest. Jay too closed his eyes. When he opened them Arlen Grasser was back at the front deep in conversation with his three companions.

Jay drifted off again. It had been an exhausting few months: the campaign, several victory parties, sorting out his staff and now trying to find his way around the nation's capital. It wasn't until the jet's engines changed tone and they began to descend that he awoke. The ground was now brown and barren. They had been flying for almost six hours. As he was watching the features below become steadily more distinct the Senator retuned and leant across him.

"Keep looking down son. There's something I want you to see."

With the Senator's face now almost pressed against his, Jay stared hard, but all he could identify was mile upon mile of the same rugged ground they had been flying over.

"There, you see that!" the Senator exclaimed.

Coming into view Jay started to pick out row after row of timber framed blocks, forming what looked like a camp or perhaps a barracks of some sort.

"That, Congressman is one of what my fine senatorial colleague Milo M Meadows the Third calls his hospitality centers," the Senator explained. "It is how the Nationalists plan to sweep up the flotsam and jetsam of this mighty mess we are in."

As the concentration of structures passed from view Jay turned to the Senator who was now standing beside him, his head not far from the cabin roof.

"You mean internment camps?"

"Hospitality centers son," he answered with a laugh. "Now I must go and relieve myself of all the coffee this fine young lady has been pouring down me. We'll be landing shortly."

CHAPTER 19

"So where are we?" Jay asked.

"What you just saw was five miles north of Las Vegas."

"Las Vegas?" Jay repeated with surprise.

"Las Vegas New Mexico, son, where Jessie James, Billy the Kid, Wyatt Earp and Doc Holliday all once hung out," the Senator elaborated. "You can't say Senator Meadows is lackin' in humor."

Ten minutes later the Gulfstream touched down on a small airstrip tucked between the folds of some rugged hills. Gena, who clearly knew more than she had been prepared to admit, told him to wait while the others disembarked. Someone, she said, would be along shortly to collect him.

* * *

"Congressman Chandler?"

A crisp young man in military uniform appeared at the door of the plane and Jay got up to meet his minder.

"Lieutenant Kurt Lang, Sir. Welcome to Los Alamos."

They shook hands although Jay suspected the soldier would have preferred a salute. As they left Gena pointed out that it was ten in the morning mountain time and that they would be flying out promptly at two that afternoon. His watch already showed one. Now thoroughly disoriented, the Lieutenant could have said 'welcome to Mars, Sir' and he would have gone along with it.

"I thought we'd go to the Bradbury Science Museum first, Sir," Lieutenant Lang proposed as they climbed into his jeep. "It has some pretty cool stuff."

The Lieutenant was right. It did. In the lobby visitors were told about the Los Alamos Facility's role in advanced research and how it was helping to improve the quality of life for the people in northern New Mexico. In the Defense Gallery its role in keeping Americans safe from chemical, biological and nuclear attack was stressed. Jay gazed at mockups of the Little Boy and Fat Man bombs dropped on Hiroshima and then Nagasaki. He knew that the first had killed some 100,000 people and that the second had probably led to the death of 80,000 more. It was only after the second that the Japanese had surrendered. It was certainly better to be on the delivering rather than the receiving end of these scientific wonders.

They moved through the History Gallery and then the Research Gallery, ending up in a little room called the Techlab where the wonders of science were displayed on a large screen. It was all interactive and fun and Lieutenant Lang was clearly proud of his nation's achievements. Jay was torn between awe, excitement, pride and the hideous responsibility, barely mentioned, that went with what was on display. It was like an arcade in which all you had to lose was what you had to pay in order to play and in the Bradbury what you had to pay was nothing.

CHAPTER 19

"Pretty interesting, Sir, don't you think?" the Lieutenant urged when they had withdrawn to a nearby Starbucks for some coffee.

Jay agreed and they talked. Kurt Lang had come from Lubbock Texas and liked the heat but missed the music often played in the Buddy Holly Center, named after one of its own. Jay asked about Alpha-Omega and sensed that this made the Lieutenant uncomfortable: his 'I know nothing about that, Sir' suggested he did, but Jay didn't pursue it. The soldier wanted to know about Congress and how decisions got made and Jay told him he was still trying to work that out himself. His guide was easy company and they got on.

"Shall we take the jeep up into the hills?" Kurt suggested, looking at his watch and for the first time dropping the 'Sir'. "We have time."

Jay said yes and they headed off up a steep track behind the town. It was rougher country than he was used to at the ranch. There was no grazing for cattle and instead a lot of sagebrush with its camphorous smell along with scrub oak, wild rose, a few cacti and rocks. Dust swirled away behind them in thick billows. Kurt Lang was obviously pleased to be heading into the back country courtesy of Uncle Sam. After bumping along, precipitously at times, they reached the tree line where the ponderosa pine started and Kurt stopped the car at what he said was the seven thousand foot level so that they could take in the view.

Away to the northeast, over the Rio Grande and beyond a wide stretch of scrub and desert, lay the city of Santa Fe, to the south the Valles Caldera, but what caught his eye were a large cluster of buildings to the west of Los Alamos embedded within the folds of the surrounding hills.

"What goes on there?" he asked.

"That's the place you were asking about," Kurt told him. "It's General Gatling's kingdom. You flew in with him."

"Alpha-Omega?"

Kurt looked at his watch.

"We'd better be heading back," he said, "otherwise I'll be on the fast track to becoming a private."

Jay took the obvious hint. Alpha-Omega wasn't to be the topic of any conversation, at least any conversation between a congressional freshman and an army lieutenant. They bounced back, locked inside their own thoughts as the town with its strange history rose up to meet them. When they reached it the ordinariness of the place struck him as banal. A habitation where it was a toss up between a skinny latte and a thermo-nuclear explosion: take your pick and enjoy. They were soon alongside the plane and Jay bid his minder goodbye, the gulf between them reestablished.

"Where have you been?" Gena asked. "You're covered in dust!"

Jay retreated back to the top step and flapped at his trousers while the attendant did her best with a brush.

"There," she said, allowing him back in. "I don't think

they'll throw you off now."

Back in his seat and with some juice Gena had brought him he reflected briefly on that moment of intimacy, but quickly banished the thought. Choosing between the high road and the side road that still lay ahead was going to be trying enough.

* * *

Just after two, mountain time – it was already past five at home – Senator Grasser clambered aboard, this time with only the suited man in tow.

"Here you are son. Your lady can now become a high priestess in her own right."

The Senator stood beaming as Jay checked the contents of the folder and saw that the crucial signature of John Franks was in place.

"Professor Franks now works here then?" Jay queried.

"We can't have our scientists running off now can we Congressman? There's work to be done for our great nation. We just don't want them telling us what to be-leeve in."

"Alpha-Omega?" Jay enquired tentatively.

The Senator, who had clearly had a successful and well-lubricated visit roared with laughter.

"Senator Milo Meadows the Third, or as my Irish friends

would say, da turd, shouldn't have all the fun now, should he Congressman? So let's just say Alpha-Omeega is a hospitality center for those with brains to offer. Brains without sense more often than not," he added with a rich rumble of delight.

"Well thank you Senator," Jay said, tapping the folder.

"My pleasure son. Now why don't you join us for some cards later?" the Senator proposed as Gena ushered him toward his seat so that the plane could take off.

As they headed away from the setting sun and back into the darkness, something of a party atmosphere developed inside the Grumman. The bourbon flowed, the cards were dealt and even Gena was persuaded to play until she had to withdraw to the galley to prepare the evening meal. She didn't drink and neither did Mr. Green, the enigmatic label attached to the third man, and Jay gave up trying to match his senior glass for glass as his wallet gradually emptied more often than not in favor of the senator who plied them with one wicked story after another about his colleagues. If the Capitol was anything it was a gossip factory, but a gossip factory with bite. Jay suspected that deals were cut and compromises made when the weaker animals had been drunk senseless or simply worn out. Green fascinated him. The man's expression gave nothing away and his reed-like voice was strangely mesmerizing. Jay was sure this inscrutable passenger could have taken the senator several times had he chosen to, just as the senator had clearly chosen to let Gena end her period of play ahead. Poker was a strange game: a mixture of luck and subterfuge toward diverse ends. His role was to lose.

The meal was served with wine after which Senator Grasser

retired to snooze on the sofa where he remained until the plane began its descent toward Andrews. Jay watched the politician's chest rise and fall in a steady rhythm suggesting peaceful contentment. That was what power looked like he realized and hoped that one day he would attain it.

On arrival Senator Grasser and his traveling companion were first to disembark into the limousine that had pulled up alongside the steps. He would have to walk through the building and locate his own car, so he talked to Gena for a while as she finished up, offering her a ride back into DC which she declined saying the co-pilot and captain were heading her way. Jay imagined flight attendants, like nurses, were always being propositioned and so needed to have escape plans ready. It had been a long shift though and tiredness had led her into one breach of protocol. In answer to a question she had let slip that Mr. Green was actually Attorney General Seymour Stone. Driving home he marveled at a day it would take him some time to make sense of.

CHAPTER 19

20

AFTER they had spoken briefly on the telephone, Marjory Anhauser told Jay to come round. He arrived to find the Chronicle's editor, Sherman Parish, already there. It was after six and the Anhauser butler had laid out drinks on a side table. Owner and editor were each holding a glass when he was shown in.

"You know Sherman, Jay, don't you?" Marjory asked.

Jay agreed that they had met and the two men shook hands.

"Help yourself to something," she encouraged "and then come and tell us what you have discovered."

"Hardly discovered," he qualified as he approached an array of spirits picking gin, mixing it with tonic and adding ice and lemon. "Senator Grasser knew exactly what he was doing," he maintained, adding as he came back to join them, "I am just not sure that I know what that was."

"Sherm, you know Arlen," Marjory said. "Where do you think he is at the moment; politically I mean?"

"We are hardly close Marjory. I have interviewed him many times, usually at his invitation when he has wanted to get some point of view out into the public domain. He's certainly one of the most effective operators on the Hill."

"He and the President have a relationship don't they?" she declared.

"Senator Grasser has a relationship with everyone who has power," Sherman laughed. "But my sense is that he is trying to work the President's agenda. That said, he and Milo Meadows are old sparring partners and often end up getting things done together."

"Jay, tell Sherm about your trip," she invited. "You had your chief of staff ask around about Alpha-Omega, right? And it all seemed to start from there. Where did this Alpha-Omega come from by the way? You said there was that girl you were trying to help."

In Marjory Anhauser's eyes any marriageable female he was associated with who was not Geraldine Cooke was relegated to the category of 'that girl'.

CHAPTER 20

"Yes, I was trying to locate a professor who ran the Center for Applied Physics until it was closed down. A friend of mine needed him to sign off on her dissertation so that she could be awarded her doctorate. He'd simply disappeared and it was suggested that he might be associated with something called Alpha-Omega."

"Could that suggestion have come from Dean Jimbalaya?" Marjory enquired, more out of curiosity than out of any desire for recrimination. She liked to know what her creatures were up to.

"I believe it might have," Jay dissembled, not wishing to breach a confidence or irritate his patron.

"Does Alpha-Omega mean anything to you Sherm?" she asked.

"In the Book of Revelation God says I am the Alpha and the Omega, the first and last letters of the Greek alphabet, the beginning and the end."

"I am not after a theology lesson," the owner of his newspaper teased.

"Of course not Marjory, but it has significance. I have heard that there is a government program that seeks to harness science to the idea of God being the beginning and the end, although I fear there may be a degree of cynicism attached to it. I should mention that many other entities have also used the name, from a Jewish dental practice to a winery just north of here that makes a pretty good Cabernet Sauvignon."

CHAPTER 20

"So the President knows about it?" she asked.

"It is hard to see how he can't," he told her.

"So tell Sherman what you learned Jay," she demanded.

"Not a lot. But it seems to be a large complex outside Los Alamos run by a General Gatling in which physicists have found employment. Senator Grasser described it rather colorfully as a Hospitality Center for those with brains, which brings me to an even more troubling revelation and why I think he had me join him on the flight to New Mexico.

"We were ten minutes or so into our descent when the senator had me look out of the window. At first I couldn't see anything other than arid desert but then a sprawling encampment came into view: row upon row of what one can only describe as huts, the sort used to confine prisoners in the Second World War. The senator made a point of telling me that what I was looking at was one of Milo Meadows's Hospitality Centers where his fellow senator planned to send the dispossessed if the Nationalists came to power."

"And where was this?" Sherman Parish asked with a heightened interest tinged with alarm.

"I remember him telling me it was north of Las Vegas, New Mexico," Jay told him.

"That's conveniently out of the way," the editor remarked.

"How can he get away with something like this?" Marjory wondered. "These places must cost even if they are primitive."

CHAPTER 20

"There have recently been some large appropriations for military encampments in several economic backwaters," Sherman told them. "Such things tend to get nodded through."

"Arlen Grasser must have known about these so-called centers," Marjory asserted.

"Hedging his bets," Sherman Parish quipped. "But the fact that he wanted you to see them Jay suggests he needed Meadows's help with Alpha-Omega but was not entirely happy with the prospect of having a quarter of the population interned, even if doing so would please most of the remaining three quarters."

"We've got to get this out Sherm," Marjory pleaded. "It might have taken us forty-six years to apologize to Japanese Americans interned during the Second World War for what we did to them, but surely people would be appalled now? And the scale! We're talking about millions not just a hundred thousand or so."

"When times are bad, Marjory," the editor told her, "people can turn a blind eye to some pretty awful things if they are persuaded that doing so will be in their best interests. If nothing else, history has taught us that."

The conversation continued for another hour or so touching on how best to verify what Jay had seen, on when to break the news if it was confirmed and on how on earth to get the dispossessed to vote when it seemed that many of them had detached themselves from a system that had detached itself from them. When the Chronicle's editor finally left Jay held back. He had unfinished business. But his hostess preempted him.

CHAPTER 20

"Now Jay," she said, "what are we going to do about this student of yours?"

"Make sure she gets her degree," Jay answered.

"I'll call Dean Jimbalaya in the morning," she assured him.

As he headed home she asked that he say 'Hi' to Geraldine. Her inference was hardly subtle, but it was clear. It was dawning on him that in life as in politics everything was an exchange of interests for mutual gain. The trick was to secure more than one lost. But the real skill, which he was learning from Arlen Grasser, lay in changing the context within which life was led so that one's opponent's small loss was transformed into a disaster and one's own small gain became a triumph. The question for now though was whose was going to be which?

* * *

Carrie and her parents flew to Newark and hired a car for their drive to the university. Commencement was one of the best celebrations in the academic calendar. Degrees were awarded and years of effort and expenditure bore the fruit hoped for although not for everyone. Some had buckled under the pressure, others had simply decided that they had better things to do with their lives than study and a few had failed to attain the standard required. Carrie herself had almost been thwarted on a technicality: instead of the Mauna Kea research center she had ended up working at Walmart in Gilroy for the want of a signature.

And even now it was not entirely straightforward. Science degrees were no longer awarded by her university for science

CHAPTER 20

alone. Since the Center for Applied Physics (CAP) had become part of the Marjory Anhauser Theological Institute (MATI) all degree courses included modules on the moral consequences of the underlying subject. Knowledge was no longer morally neutral, to be pursued regardless of its potential consequences. There had been great advances in genetics at the university but whether or not the human genome should be altered had become a topic of intense debate. Even undergraduates learning how to develop computer games were now being forced to consider the ethics of online violence.

None of this had been included in Carrie's degree courses and Dean Jimbalaya was anxious not to undermine the school's new image by being seen to award a degree on the old basis. Had Marjory Anhauser not signaled her desire to see the degree conferred he would have insisted that Ms. Holden complete the additional courses. He'd contemplated awarding her an honorary doctorate but age was against this. Instead she would be processed along with three students earning degrees in metaphysics and he hoped no one outside the university would notice.

Carrie and her parents drove south on the New Jersey Turnpike past highly automated plants that employed few people and which in any event were operating at well below capacity. Blackouts had become more frequent all the way down the Eastern seaboard as operators cut back on maintenance to conserve cash flow and cover the dividends they were expected to pay to the retirees who depended on them. It was becoming a vicious circle. Under pressure from politicians, the Federal Reserve had pumped money into the economy in the hope that this would stimulate activity. But all it had done was eviscerate the income of savers, forcing a steady stream of them to join the ranks of the dispossessed.

In open country beyond the industrial zone they passed clusters of what looked like tented hamlets. Over to their left was Staten Island where the Dutch had tried several times unsuccessfully to settle. An Italian explorer had been the first European to record its existence in 1520 but the Dutch had persevered and eventually established themselves in 1661 against often fierce opposition from the local Lenape Indians whose land it was. The Dutch had not had it their own way for long. After the Anglo-Dutch war the place had been ceded to the English in 1667 becoming part of that nation's New York colony. None of this the Holdens knew, which was probably just as well as they might have thought they were traveling back in time, a concept familiar to Carrie although over light years, not centuries.

By the time they got to Adams on Highway 1 things started to look more normal with neat groups of shops selling necessaries together with fast food from one or other of the chains which continued to earn money on account of their value. The auto-lots were still loaded with cars but how many were selling was impossible to say. They turned off the highway onto the county road and crossed over Carnegie Lake built by the great Scottish-born industrialist so that university boat crews had somewhere to practice. As it happened, the university's direction had largely been set by another Scot, a Presbyterian minister, John Witherspoon, who had spent much of his life attempting to reconcile secular and moral issues, so in reality the institution was returning to its roots.

When they reached the campus it was as if they had entered a different world: calm and peaceful and underpinned by large

CHAPTER 20

donations from past industrial plutocrats, although even the university was finding it hard to finance all its obligations. Madge and Bill Holden might not have known much about what their daughter had studied but they were quietly bursting with pride at her achievement. Carrie took them to one of the campus cafés until it was time for them to take their seats in the hall while she went off to gown up. There had been days when she wondered if this moment would ever come and wished that Jay could have been there to witness it, having done so much to bring it about.

The proceedings went off without a hitch, as they usually did, although she was sad to have been the only pure physicist getting a degree. In the center of the robed 'wise people' on the podium sat Dean Jimbalaya and Marjory Anhauser. The three getting their doctorates in metaphysics she had been grouped with were as curious about her as she was about them, but there was little time to talk. For them the nature of reality was up for debate; for her it was supposed to be an observable fact, although in the quantum world the nature of reality was proving hard to pin down. In everyday life, however, she was happy to concede that context did determine how facts were conceived.

An alumna, Doreen Studebaker, who was currently leader of the Moralists in the Senate, gave the commencement address. She reminded the graduates that they were part of a coherent whole for which God was a perfectly good metaphor and that they should not pursue their interests without thinking long and hard about the effect it might have on that whole. There would, she warned them, be many occasions when self-interest drew them away from that consideration. "So develop a moral compass," she urged her audience; "because," she said "you will need it."

CHAPTER 20

21

SANFORD Dodge worked at the Mount Nittany Medical Center. At the weekend he liked to walk his Russell Terrier, Millie, in the Millbrook Marsh area nearby. His Sunday routine was fixed. coffee and a donut at Dunkin' and then an hour with Millie. It wasn't perhaps the best place to exercise a dog as she always came back wet and often muddy, but since Mrs. Dodge's passing Millie had become the center of his domestic life. Walks were invariably followed by a wash in the tub, all of which helped fill the day.

Having not thought much about such things in the past, Sanford had become a keen conservationist. The creeks that crisscrossed the area, fed in part by runoff from the nearby Tussey

Mountain and in part by underground springs, were returning to their pristine state thanks to local efforts. Surrounding development had been held in check and the little stream that Millie liked to run alongside and frequently splash into was still a crystal clear thoroughfare for trout and the generous source of fresh drinking water for those who lived nearby.

He'd been a Rationalist all his life: after all his profession had been built upon the rigorous application of knowledge. But when Mrs. Dodge contracted cancer and the treatment he had insisted upon started to degrade the life that she had left, he was forced to come to terms with the limitations of his vocation. Scientific research had done much, he was the first to recognize, but it could not solve every problem and it could not tell people how to live or die. In his deep attachment to reason he had become blind to life as it was with its random beginnings, unpredictable middles and certain ends. Without a belief in the whole as a shared mystery individual life lost its meaning. His wife's death had taught him that.

And it had not stopped there. The Center had let two of his colleagues 'go' in order to bring expenditure and income back into balance. The pair had been no worse, in any objective sense, than anyone else who worked there, just less connected to the governing committee and a plausible reason was concocted for their selection. Neither had found jobs and he knew that the younger of the two was now living with his wife and child in one of the encampments that had sprung up in parks around the city. The Millbrook Marsh was unsuitable for such sites, which was perhaps why he picked it to exercise Millie. He had no idea where the second person had gone and had made no effort to find out.

CHAPTER 21

But he had resolved to support Henry Dukes and the Moralist platform at the next election.

They were near the top end when Millie found something to absorb her in the thick undergrowth. He walked on, confident she would reappear and catch him up. But she didn't and so he walked back to where he had last seen her and began to call.

"Millie, come girl," he shouted, "we haven't got all day!" They probably did; he just wasn't keen to spend what was left of it waiting for her.

"Millie girl; come, come, come!"

He tried a whistle but it was mostly air that left his lips. He had always been envious of those like the doormen at fancy hotels who could hail a cab at fifty paces with the shrill of a steam engine.

"Come here Millie. I'm serious."

He assumed that she was sensitive to his mood, but if that was the case she had found something more absorbing.

After several minutes of unrequited demands he started to worry. Was she caught, trapped under a root, perhaps in the water? His mild anger turned into real concern. He studied the terrain beyond the trail. It looked hostile: full of tangled vines and appeared soggy under foot. Where to start? He had just taken his first step when Millie shot out of the thicket a few yards from where he was standing and raced up to him with her customary enthusiasm which generally defused any anger he had. She had something in her mouth which she dropped at his feet – it was a human finger.

He stared at it, unbelieving at first and moved the object with his shoe. But it remained a human finger.

Millie stood by, eager and panting.

"Jesus, Millie. What have you found?" he muttered while Millie barked taking a few steps away and then a few steps back as if enticing him to follow her.

"OK girl, you'd better show me," he said, moving toward her which she took as her cue to run back into the undergrowth, yapping as she went.

The brambles clawed at him and he felt moisture seeping into his boots which sunk into the mud. With Millie's bark to guide him he persevered and must have been fifty yards in when he saw the body. It was that of a well-dressed woman now disheveled and damp and starting to seep into the vegetation around it. He couldn't see her face, only her hair matted black against the moss. Her arm had been pulled out from under her by her now chewed hand which was one finger short. The smell coming from the disturbed body left him in no doubt that what he was looking at was dead.

Sanford called the police on his mobile while Millie danced up and down eager to take at least some of her discovery home for dinner. This was not going to be a normal Sunday.

CHAPTER 21

* * *

Henry Dukes was in a blind fury. The death of Freja Olsen, assumed to be murder, had hit the headlines in every newspaper. The Nationalist press was pointing the finger squarely at the two students from the religious college and even the Rationalist- and Moralist- inclined organs were being circumspect in their judgment.

A young, female, well-respected foreign academic, invited to the United States to present a paper, had been found dead in a nature reserve. Those facts were irrefutable. One religious journal tried to hoist a trial balloon suggesting that the lady might have had mental problems so that suicide could not be ruled out, but under heavy institutional fire from both sides of the Atlantic that inflated speculation fell to earth in flames like the Hindenburg. The more lurid branches of the media even conjectured that the young female professor had been sexually abused as well as killed and that was before the results of any post mortem had been made public. For several days a flotilla of newshounds had been stationed outside the home of a Pennsylvania widower who one network managed to misname as Sanford Dog, confusing the man with his animal. Blanketed under this blizzard of innuendo and half truth and with an election looming, White House staffers were in meltdown.

"Eunice, have you got the Attorney General yet?"

"I have been trying Mr. President, but he's not picking up."

"Well <u>keep</u> trying Eunice."

CHAPTER 21

"Yes Mr. President."

"And have you got the Governor. I need to speak to the Governor."

"I have spoken to his office but he has not called back yet. They assure me he will just as soon as they can reach him."

"Oh bullshit! What goddamn Governor can't be reached by his office?"

"Perhaps he's talking to Attorney Stone," the President's secretary suggested with a hint of chastisement in reaction to his manner.

The tension was close to breaking point when Eunice announced that she had Governor Thompson on the line and the President got straight to the point.

"Governor, I want to know what you are doing with those two boys…."

"I appreciate that justice must take its course Governor, but the Attorney General is telling me this was a student prank that was hijacked by other parties…."

"No I don't know who the other parties were, but I can hazard a guess…."

"I know this is not a goddamn guessing game Governor, but lynching these boys without evidence would be nigger justice Northern Style…."

CHAPTER 21

"How do you mean you have no evidence that any other parties were involved? What evidence do you have that the boys did the killing?...."

"Now don't electric chair me, Governor. Of course the public want this resolved...."

"You know I can't even think about clemency right before an election, any more than you can. Besides, the wheels of justice must be allowed to turn first, and I mean - wheels of justice. When will we get the results of the autopsy?...."

"Well keep me informed ..."

"I appreciate that."

Henry was blue with anger after finishing the call. The Governor had been elected on the Rationalist ticket but was known to have Nationalist leanings. From what he had learned of the Millbrook affair so far, the two students had been half-witted but it seemed unlikely they were murderers. Of course the prank could have gone wrong and the woman could have just died or been killed by some freak accident causing the boys to panic. At present that was at least as plausible as a Nationalist conspiracy, perhaps more so unless you knew what the Nationalists were capable of and he felt he was beginning to.

Eunice came in with a fresh pot of coffee and filled his mug.

"I can't stand that man," he said.

CHAPTER 21

"Thompson?"

"Yes, Thompson," he told her. "He came right out a while back and said my Home Stabilization Initiative was not just socialist nonsense, but communist evil. He's the sort of politician who would like to send every one of the dispossessed to some penal colony and call the problem solved. Balancing supply and demand he would call it, an idea growing in popularity I am afraid to say."

"That's just awful, Mr. President."

"That it is, Eunice. That it is. Now where the hell's my Attorney?"

It was hard to concentrate on anything else but the office he occupied and wanted to remain in for another four years was not conducive to navel-gazing. At least the Middle East was no longer the priority it had been. The growth in shale oil and renewable energy had seen to that and with the collapse in economic activity depressing the demand for oil further, no one was paying much attention to the sheikhs and the mullahs any more. The State Department still clung to its global thinking, but the rest of the world was weaning itself off the American teat. Never slow to flex its muscles, the Pentagon continued to be on the lookout for a war it could justify (and win although its record in this regard was patchy), but the public wasn't having it. Domestic concerns overrode everything, although on that there was gridlock. The malaise would break eventually, but it was not going to be the status quo ante that emerged when it did.

He consoled himself that Lincoln had faced a similar

CHAPTER 21

situation: one nation united or two countries with radically different outlooks. The choice was again between two paths. One would lead to a whole nation morally revived, the other to a narrower totemic focus which would inevitably exclude, just as the Confederacy had done. Of course neither would be perfect, even by its own standards. What human arrangement ever was? So he had been busy working the phones, threatening, cajoling and bribing and before bed, rereading Michael Burlingame's *Abraham Lincoln: a life*.

It must have been a good hour after his round with the Governor that the intercom clicked and Eunice told him she had Attorney Stone on the line. He and Seymour talked and talked. They agreed that the Federal Bureau should be involved but Stone reminded him of his suspicion that the agency had become politicized so there was no guarantee that if there had been Nationalist involvement in the professor's death, it would emerge in an unambiguous way. Opacity would be jumped on to support the Nationalist story which seemed to be crystalizing around a call for strong leadership in the face of escalating disorder.

"We need to reign in these attacks on the academics," President Dukes urged, imagining that what he and Stone had initiated they could stop. But the Attorney wasn't having it.

"It may have gone too far for that," Stone told him. "I am pretty sure Meadows is behind most of it now. He doesn't mind who's attacked frankly as long as it generates disorder and of course he's trying to make it look as though it's coming out of these encampments."

CHAPTER 21

"Live by the sword, die by the sword," the President intoned.

"You know he's building a network of holding centers into which the dispossessed will be herded if he gains power?"

"I had heard something along those lines," the President confirmed. "And I believe he's using my General Gatling to oversee this. I wish I hadn't needed Meadows to help me set up Alpha-Omega. He's got me snookered there."

"Well perhaps not entirely," the Attorney suggested. "Senator Grasser has opened a window onto all of this and we have to hope that when the fresh air of publicity blows, it blows in the right direction and at the right moment."

"Away from Alpha-Omega and onto Meadows's so-called Hospitality Centers?"

"Exactly," Seymour Stone all but incanted.

* * *

When the results of the post mortem were released, indicating that Freja Olsen had sustained a blow to the front of her head sufficient to knock her unconscious and had died from suffocation caused by a surfeit of marsh water in her lungs, the die was cast for Matthew Fenton and Robert Hardy. The prosecutor alleged that the professor had run from her captors, hit her head on a branch and fallen unconscious face first into the swamp where she had suffocated and died. The boys' defense argued that persons unknown had dragged Freja Olsen from the car, taped and cuffed, and that that was the last they had seen of her. The jury took just over an hour to agree with the prosecution and the judge handed down an eight year prison sentence for constructive manslaughter. The Nationalist press had a field day. *Callous religious students leave young professor to die*, was a typical headline.

CHAPTER 21

CHAPTER 21

22

MARJORY Anhauser was in New York for a quarterly meeting with the financial managers of her Foundation which had lost half its value since the start of the crisis. Once again she looked forward to hearing them justify their fees. Had everything been placed in an unmanaged index fund the result would have been the same. In spite of the loss, she was determined not to cut back on the support the Foundation gave, especially to MATI. Resources were being used to underpin several Moralist candidates as well as Henry Dukes's reelection, but this entailed drawing on capital to supplement the Foundation's declining income, sowing alarm amongst her managers. If the capital expired, so would their gravy train.

Her car took her to West Street in Manhattan where her manager's plush offices were located. She was ushered through security and escorted up to the tenth floor where the senior partner, David Ovitz, was there to meet her along with the Foundation's two day-to-day account managers, John Andelman and Gail De Castro.

"Marjory, it's good to see you," David greeted. "I hope you didn't get caught up in the demonstration."

An anti-Rationalist march had briefly closed the Brooklyn Bridge until police cleared it.

"No," Marjory told him. "There were just a few stragglers on the road by the time we got there."

"Something to drink?" he asked. "We do have your mint tea this time."

"Well I had better have mint tea then," she said.

The meeting turned to the business at hand after David Ovitz and Marjory both agreed that the state of the nation was parlous and that a resolution of the political impasse was needed. Whether it was for her benefit or not she couldn't tell, but her host appeared to favor the President's plan. He said he wasn't sure about the community aspect of the initiative, but did think that reliquefying the housing market was essential. For him it was an arithmetic exercise rather than a matter of moral rejuvenation, and she saw little point in calling him out on that. It was not easy for a man who had worked hard all his life and was now earning several million dollars a year to imagine that the system he was part of was anything other than rational.

John Andelman was the first to present his report. A momentum investor who favored growth stocks, he had guided the Foundation into some spectacular successes in the past but since the crisis growth had collapsed and momentum had turned down rather than up. He methodically reported on each of his holdings.

"And why didn't you start selling, John?" his client asked when he had finished. "It had been apparent for some time that growth stocks were fully valued. We have been having this conversation for over a year now and every time you have said that the companies on your list are simply the best companies around."

"If you remember, Marjory," David interjected in support of his young colleague, "we did try to persuade you over a year ago to divert at least some of the Foundation's funds into two or three of our proprietary investments in the private, unquoted area."

"Of course I remember, David," she accepted. "But my view now is the same as it was then; such investments are illiquid and hard to value. They would sit in the account at cost and look pretty good right now, unless we had to sell any. These sorts of investments can take years to show their potential and that's assuming expectations are fulfilled."

"We were only talking about a portion of the fund, Marjory," David pointed out. "And there can be some great gains in this area."

CHAPTER 22

"And great fees for you David," she laughed.

"So would you like us to replace John then?" he asked.

"Certainly not," she countered. "By and large I agree with him. The companies on his list are great companies. And thanks to his earlier success we are still sitting on some profits. I should have insisted on this before John, but I would like you to increase cash by twenty percent right away. Hold it in short term government paper until this nightmare is over. We will review it quarter by quarter as we go forward."

Both chastened and relieved, John Andelman agreed and David Ovitz offered no resistance.

"Now tell me David, how much is John's portion down from its high? This is not shown on the summary you gave me."

"Sixty percent I believe is the figure," he announced through gritted teeth.

"And Gail's portion of the fund: how much is that down?"

"That'll be around forty percent I think," he said shifting uneasily in his seat.

"So our split between value and growth has paid off. And of course most of the Fund's free income comes from the dividends paid by the companies on Gail's list. So well done Gail, could we have your report."

Marjory enjoyed being able to praise the young lady,

CHAPTER 22

especially as it irritated David Ovitz, whose ability was matched by his sense of self-worth. In the world of commerce and even more so in that of finance, her sex was still under-represented. Besides, Gail De Castro took an interest in what the Foundation did, which she knew the other two did not and appreciated how important a steady stream of dividends was. Her challenge the young manager said, as she went through her list, was to find companies that could keep earning and paying out as the economy continued to contract.

Before the meeting broke up they talked generally about which areas would do best if the Nationalists won or the Moralists did. Even amongst its beneficiaries the Rationalist approach was losing credibility. The columnist Edward Luce had recently compared the prevailing order to the last days of old Europe before Martin Luther shook the corrupt Catholic hierarchy to its core. Luce asked how it was possible in a meritocracy for the Presidency to have frequently been a family affair and for the country's 400 richest families to be worth as much as the bottom 300 million souls combined. It seemed that fewer and fewer people were thinking that Rationalism was rational any more. While it was clear that a Nationalist administration would favor defense stocks and that a Moralist victory would be good for the banks, certainly in the short term, Marjory argued that on a longer term prognosis the Moralist approach won by a mile.

"The Nationalist agenda will lead to a very narrow focus and a top heavy economy," she maintained. "It will be like a shot of cocaine and will wear off as fast unless repeated in ever larger quantities. But if the nation can be rebuilt morally from the ground up there will be a widespread revival. It might take time as so much damage has been done, but I am sure it would come."

CHAPTER 22

David Ovitz was less sure, however it was her Foundation and he wasn't about to argue.

* * *

That evening Marjory went with a friend to see a staging of Richard Wagner's *Die Walküre* at the Metropolitan Opera House. Only two blocks from Central Park, the Lincoln Center was ablaze with lights and splendor, in sharp contrast to the encampments that had taken hold in the park itself in spite of the mayor's attempt to stop them. In the end people felt that it was the least the city could do for those who had fallen on the wrong side of the economic divide, just so long as they behaved, which for the most part they had. Grouped like villages, easy to mistake for weekend markets, these tented hamlets of a nomadic age nestling amongst honeycombs of glass and steel hinted uncomfortably at the frailty of human progress.

However in their box on the Grand Tier level Marjory and her friend could forget all of that. Opened in 1966 to entertain almost 4,000 people, the place was a marvel with its hydraulic elevators, motorized stages and rigging systems. She could see that it was not full although the standing room section at the back was: during the crisis it was being made available for free. One didn't need to have a degree in sociology, economics or any other branch of the social sciences to know that a system that could throw up such glaring contrasts was badly broken. And yet what could those inside the auditorium do other than count their blessings and assume that they had done something right and that those less fortunate had done something wrong? Elections were a blunt instrument at best and politics, for the most part, was a sport of self-interest easily gamed.

CHAPTER 22

The lights dimmed and *Wotan*, chief of the gods, was revealed in great anguish. He tells how he has tricked *Alberich* of the *Nibelung* out of the ring which is the source of wealth and power and given it to the giants, *Fafner* and *Fasolt* as ransom for *Freia*, goddess of youth and beauty, who he had promised them for building his kingdom of *Walhalla*. But *Alberich* has cursed the ring and after *Fafner* slays *Fasolt* in a squabble, *Wotan* worries that *Alberich's* curse will be visited on the gods. So he begets with *Erda*, goddess of wisdom, the *Valkyrs*, led by *Brünnhilde*, wild maidens who course through the air on superb chargers and bear the bodies of dead heroes to *Walhalla*, where they revive and aid the gods in warding off attacks by the *Nibelungs*.

But *Wotan* also needs to retrieve the curse-laden ring from the giant *Fafner* and return it to the *Rhinedaughters* from whom it was stolen. However this has to be done for entirely unselfish motives. As the gods cannot help but be selfish he casts off his divinity and has two twins, *Siegmund* a boy and *Sieglinde* a girl by an ordinary mortal in the hope that *Siegmund* will one day slay *Fafner* and return the ring to the *Rhinedaughters*. To toughen them for the task ahead they are separated and *Wotan* surrounds them with hardships.

In the opening Act, after *Wotan* has set the scene, *Siegmund*, now a young man, seeks shelter from his pursuers during a violent storm in a hut belonging to the robber *Hunding* who *Sieglinde* has been forced to marry. *Siegmund* and *Sieglinde* are immediately attracted to one another. *Hunding* returns and reveals that he has been one of *Siegmund's* pursuers and says that while he can stay the night, they must fight in the morning. *Sieglinde* drugs *Hunding's* drink with a sleeping potion and reveals to *Siegmund* that she has been forced into the marriage. She tells him that an old man has left a sword that will protect her embedded in a tree which only a hero can remove. *Siegmund* withdraws the sword without difficulty and in talking about their past they realize they are brother and sister and *Sieglinde* succumbs to *Siegmund's* love.

As the first Act drew to a close Marjory reflected on the great gulf between the rational world of science and the emotional world of actual human experience. She found herself wondering which came closest to reality: the ancient Norse myths captured by Wagner or the pure science of the physicists. Was our lust for knowledge not a little like *Alberich's* lust for the ring? But before she could tie herself into knots over this, the second Act began.

Anxious that *Siegmund* should win his contest against *Hunding, Wotan* sends his *Valkyrie* daughter, *Brünnhilde* to help him, an instruction he cancels when he learns that *Siegmund* and *Sieglinde* have consummated their love. But *Brünnhilde* is moved by this love and decides to defy her father and help *Siegmund* in the battle. *Wotan* realizes what is going on and shatters *Siegmund's* sword, allowing *Hunding* to kill him, but then he kills *Hunding* while *Brünnhilde* rides off with *Sieglinde*.

In the final act the *Valkyrs* try to protect *Brünnhilde* from the wrath of *Wotan* but they are too weak and *Wotan* tells *Brünnhilde* that she will be left on a mountain for any passing man who wants her. But after listening to her tell him that she understood his true wish for *Siegmund* he relents and resolves to cast a circle of fire round her on the mountain which only a hero will be able to penetrate.

As the final Act of the production concludes a wild *Fury* appears to tell the audience how the story ends. *Sieglinde*, she sings, gives birth to *Siegfried*, her and *Siegmund's* son. The boy is reared in the forest where *Fafner* guards the sacred token. *Siegfried* eventually finds his father's sword, pieces it together and slays *Fafner*, regaining the ring. He then penetrates the circle of fire around *Brünnhilde* and they fall in love. But *Hagen*, son of *Alberich,* plots his downfall. *Siegfried* is fed a potion that makes him forget *Brünnhilde*. Furious, she allows *Hagen* to kill him before learning of *Hagen's* treachery.

Distraught at being so duped, her deep love for *Siegfried* overcomes her earlier rage. The goddess draws the ring from his finger and throws herself into a pyre she herself has lit. As the flames rise all around destroying not only *Brünnhilde* but *Walhalla*, land of the gods, one of the *Rhinedaughters*, protected by water, swims in and reclaims the ring stolen from them. Through love, the emotion rejected by *Alberich* to gain wealth and power, *Brünnhilde* has caused the old order to collapse and a new era to begin.

As the curtain descended and the applause died away, an anxious official came onto the stage.

"Can I have your attention, please: your attention."

He had to plead several times before the surprised spectators turned their attention on him.

"While the performance has been in progress," he announced, "there have been riots outside in the Lincoln Center. The police have now largely dealt with the protestors but we would ask you to be on your guard as you leave the building. We have opened the side and back exits and would encourage as many who can to use them. Thank you for coming and we hope that this will not spoil what I am sure you will all agree has been an outstanding evening."

Spontaneously the now nervous audience applauded the announcer almost as heartily as it had applauded the opera company.

Marjory and her friend had coats to collect and so had to wait in line by one of the cloakrooms above the main foyer. At least those with boxes were served by their own and so she hoped the wait would not be long. Like her friend, Marjory was still partly locked inside Wagner's *Der Ring des Nibelungen*, written as four dramas but performed that evening as one, now conflated with the drama that had been going on outside, when she became aware of a powerful looking man approaching her.

"Mrs. Anhauser!" he proclaimed. "I thought it was you. I was with friends in a box opposite and wanted to come round and pay my respects."

Marjory stared at the man without any immediate recognition, as one does when confronted by a person out of context.

"Milo Meadows," the man prompted. "We met at a fundraiser for injured veterans, two years ago I think it was, in the capital."

The name was enough to bring Marjory's concentration sharply down to earth.

"Oh, Senator Meadows! Of course I know exactly who you

are. Perhaps you were in the cast this evening as Wotan!"

"Sadly ma'am, I can't sing. But I would like to think that we could work together, at least until some order has been brought back into our great nation. Pandora's Box has been opened. Wild men are roaming the country and no one is safe."

"So neither I imagine are you, Senator."

"Possibly good lady, possibly. But there is much anger around and it can erupt at anytime, anywhere. Anyway, I just wanted to pay my respects."

With that he gave her a slight bow and disappeared back to where he had come from.

"Wasn't that Senator Meadows?" her friend asked excitedly as she rejoined the coats line from the cloakroom.

"Yes," Marjory answered tersely, "it was."

"What did he want?"

"Oh just to deliver a message from the gods, I think." But her friend was still trying to make sense in her head of the epic they had witnessed and had no capacity left to unravel this answer.

As she left the building Marjory was shocked by what she saw. A beautiful public space had been trashed. She felt real anger, the sort of anger Milo Meadows was depending upon to carry him into power. Red paint had been smeared on many of the

CHAPTER 22

buildings, the fountain was full of the detritus of protest – twisted barriers, beaten up waste bins, even a pram, although there was no sign of a baby - and groups of police were still hanging around in full riot gear looking edgy after the battle they had fought and won. Marjory hastened past the Koch Theater, jaywalking across West 62nd Street into Fordham University where a car was waiting to take her back to the hotel. She went to sleep that night wondering whether the illusion of certainty sown by science in the human mind had caused men and women to mislay wisdom.

* * *

She'd had things to do and people to see in New York and hadn't flown out of Newark until after five the following afternoon. But by Pacific Time it wasn't even nine in the evening when her driver carried her suitcase into the house.

"Will there be anything else, Mrs. Anhauser?" he asked.

"No Arthur, thank you. That will be all."

Augusta was there to make a fuss of her. It was good to be home. Later, before retiring, she sat next to her cathedral window as she often did just to take in the view. It was a clear night. There was no fog. The Point Bonita Lighthouse was at work sending out its rhythmic message. The bridge was lit. Below on China Beach she could see a fire sparking upward whenever someone poked it. Kids, she imagined. They often went there to hang out. But what if it wasn't? For a moment she felt the fear Milo Meadows had wanted her to feel.

CHAPTER 22

23

HENRY and Mary Dukes were unaware of the three shots that had been fired hitting a member of their security detail and a cheering well-wisher as they left the Cervantes Convention Center, named after a former mayor of St Louis, Alfonso J Cervantes, thought by some to have had connections with organized crime but regarded by others as a man who loved his city and got things done. The rally had gone well. The President was running neck and neck in the polls with Milo M Meadows III who was pushing his law and order agenda. Henry felt that his Home Stabilization Initiative was popular enough but that the Moralist argument was not resonating as well as he had hoped. His big problem was that the main beneficiaries of his program had all but dropped out of the political system: they were not attending his rallies and the pollsters were finding them unresponsive.

It was the First Lady's "Oh my God!" that alerted Henry to the drama unfolding around him, an alert amplified by his being manhandled along with Mrs. Dukes into their waiting limousine.

"What the hell's going on?" he shouted as he was shoved unceremoniously onto the back seat with Mary all but thrown on top of him: his defenders had their priorities.

"A shooter, Mr. President," an agent shouted from the front seat as the car sped off.

"Anyone get hit?" Henry called back as he struggled to right himself from under the First Lady.

"Agent Stimson got it."

"Killed?"

"We don't know."

"What is this country <u>coming</u> to Henry?" Mary protested. "At least six presidents have been shot at, and four successfully." She had been doing her research.

"That's democracy Mary!" her husband retorted, now enjoying something of an adrenaline rush. "People feel they have a right to hire and fire."

"I don't think that's funny Henry," snapped Mary. "There

is something called <u>the law</u>."

"The law is only what people choose to defend dear," he answered distractedly as he strained to hear a message being relayed over the radio.

"Stimson's going to make it," their agent relayed back to them, "but a lady in the crowd got hit twice."

"Be sure to find out where they're being taken," the President instructed. "We should visit. And make damn sure there are no cameras: this is a private matter, if one is allowed such things anymore."

"Yes it's even hard to be a secret agent these days," their minder remarked, without a hint of irony.

"Has the shooter been apprehended?" the President asked.

"I haven't heard that he has," the man reported.

"Well he obviously wasn't a very good shot," the President quipped.

"Henry, really!"

* * *

Back on Air Force One there was an atmosphere of studied panic. The phone relay from the White House was alive with calls from various members of the government who had seen news reports of the shooting.

CHAPTER 23

"Get me my secretary," the President barked as soon as he was on board.

The emergency protocol was in full swing.

"That's her now, Mr. President," an aide responded.

"No, we're both fine Eunice. But an agent was hit as well as a lady in the crowd, twice I think. We were just leaving the convention center...."

"Can you tell all callers we are fine, but I do want to speak to Attorney General Stone...."

"He did, well have him call me again. We are off to Kansas City now as planned. The American people need to be reassured – or disappointed!" he added with a laugh, out of earshot of Mrs. Dukes....

"And Eunice, we'll be adjusting our schedule and flying back briefly to St. Louis tonight: Mary and I want to visit the two people who **were** shot. Will you arrange flowers...."

"No, I don't know where they've been taken. The news channels will probably know before I do...."

"Yes, we will Eunice. Thank you."

As the Boeing 747-9 climbed out of Missouri the military on board were in contact with their ground stations to ascertain if the shooting had wider implications. The Vice President had been alerted in case the presidential plane itself was attacked. Out

CHAPTER 23

of the window those on board could see two fighter jets alongside scrambled from the Whiteman Air Force Base.

"Mr. President," an aide called out, "I have the Attorney General."

Henry took himself off to a quiet corner of the plane and picked up one of the phones.

"Seymour...."

"No, we are both fine...."

"The question is, was this some lone goofball or something more sinister...."

"I should at least get a sympathy bounce in the polls out of it, so if it was part of someone's great plan they picked a lousy marksman...."

"I agree, but Meadows's order-disorder thing is gaining traction and he's making me look impotent. That's not good Seymour: not good at all. People want a leader who is on top of things and right now, thanks to the gridlock in Congress, I don't look as though I can tie my own shoe laces...."

"Quite...."

"Well if this goes on much longer, I'm going to have to take a leaf out of the Nationalist playbook and declare war on some goddamn dictator just to enhance my CV...."

CHAPTER 23

"See what you can unearth then and keep me posted."

'Keep me posted' was a figure of speech, as he and his Attorney General both knew. There were certain things a president did not need to find in his post box.

* * *

The rally in Kansas City went better than expected. People had been shocked by what had happened and wanted to show their support. It was after eight when they flew back into St Louis. A car took them straight to University Hospital. They found Agent Roger Stimson sitting up in bed. The bullet had passed through his shoulder and not even broken a bone. He and Mary talked with him for a while and he thanked them for the flowers. When Mary was out of the room being taken to the other victim, Henry asked him how he thought the shooter had missed his target and the agent's answer was troubling.

"Perhaps he hadn't," he said. "Perhaps he just wanted to stir up confusion."

But it was what he said next that chilled.

"I probably shouldn't be saying this, Mr. President. But there is a rumor going round inside the agency that there is a cell working to support the Nationalists."

Henry stared at him in utter disbelief.

"As I say, Mr. President, it is just a rumor. But if a cell exists, it won't get me. My brother has a young wife and two small children and they are living in a tent right now. He was laid off and they lost everything, so I am rooting for your program."

Henry thanked him for his service and went to join Mary. What he had just heard he would not share with her. The second victim was on life support. Her name was Julia Somerset and she was a student activist for the Moralist cause. When Henry arrived Mary was with the girl's parents in the ante-room. They all talked for a while about the inconsequential things that come to mind at such moments and Henry was grateful he had Mary with him. She had a touch he didn't. As they left, a nurse pulled him aside.

"There's no insurance, Mr. President," she said.

"Do whatever you can for that young lady and send your bill to the White House, marked for my attention," he told her.

At last there was something the President of the United States could actually do.

They would stay on the plane that night. It would be Omaha in the morning, Des Moines in the afternoon and Pierre, South Dakota in the evening. Mary had long ago concluded that the life of a politician was a poor one and he was beginning to agree. As he lay in the Presidential bed unable to sleep, Roger Stimson's words kept charging around his head like the Four Horsemen of the Apocalypse.

* * *

Once again Seymour Stone was on his way to Chicago's Peninsula Hotel to meet with Pietro LaBoucher. What the

CHAPTER 23

President had been told by agent Stimson had an alarming ring of truth about it. The smell of decay was everywhere. The political situation was getting worse and the drive in from the airport suggested that life on the ground was too. The encampments were more numerous as were the signs of dilapidation: neither government nor private sector was spending. 'Holding on' had become the entrenched practice so as to avoid falling into an abyss looming larger by the day. It was as if the crew of a boat approaching a fall could only argue more loudly amongst themselves to assuage their rising fear.

For Milo Meadows, however, fear was the perfect weapon. It seemed to be in the nature of those who felt lost and paralyzed to crave strong leadership. The person who could say 'follow me, I have a plan' with enough force and conviction to suggest that they actually did would Pied Piper them away like the children of Hamelin. In trying to turn economic unease against rationalism he had attempted to pull off the same trick. Now it looked as though the Nationalists had stolen his pony and trap and ditched the trap. LaBoucher was almost certainly working for both sides, but that was negotiable and why he had come back to Chicago. What alarmed him was the possibility that the Nationalists might be gaining control over the state.

"Welcome Mr. Brown," the receptionist greeted. "It's nice to have you back."

For several seconds the Attorney General forgot who he was and stared blankly at her.

"Shall I send Mr. Green right up when he arrives?"

CHAPTER 23

That prompt was enough to remind him of his limp charade. One day Mr. Brown, another day Mr. Green.

"Yes please," he replied, glancing up at the clock on the wall behind her head. "I'm not expecting him for another hour."

"Can I have someone help you with your bag?"

"No, I can manage, thank you. It's light. I'll be leaving later this evening."

"Well you have a good meeting then Mr. Brown," she said, quite inured to people's strange ways.

Seymour padded around his suite making sure everything was in order. He had an affinity with hotels, especially the good ones. Everything was always in its place and there was nothing extraneous. The perfect impersonality of their rooms appealed to him. They had remembered the jug of lemonade so he poured himself a glass and took it with him onto the balcony. He was sorry to be foregoing another meal with his guest who he did not dislike. The man was a little like himself: clear-headed, to the point; a person who took the world as it was and got things done.

It was a pleasant evening. With one hand on the rail he soaked it all in as he drank with restrained sips before putting the empty glass down on the table beside him. No one, he felt could help but be uplifted by a city at night; its dark rectangular caverns punctured by peopleless windows shining bright, all dissected by glowing arteries ferrying around the human capsules of hemoglobin that made it work. He never noticed until the last moment the two men who had entered and who then prized him

CHAPTER 23

over the barrier onto the street below.

A passing wino had seen everything, or thought he had. A few other passersby had seen or heard something, but were not sure what. The hotel doorman had been busy helping three men out of their limousine and so had missed it, although he thought he had seen a private ambulance waiting earlier but felt he must have been mistaken. The only man with a clear view of the body hitting the ground had been 'Mr. Green' who was standing next to the doorman while his two minders addressed their driver. With an instinct for such things, he had quickly got back into the vehicle, claiming they'd brought him to the wrong hotel, and been driven away.

During a lull in his duties, the doorman wandered over to where the body had been. He took the damp patch on the pavement to be the wine or urine from another wino who had drunk his last and been carted off to the city morgue. He mistook the shards of spectacle glass for those from a bottle. The living wino gibbered at him about a body flying through the sky, but the doorman told him to move on. No one had seen Mr. Green arrive or Mr. Brown leave. The bill had been prepaid. The registration had been perfunctory and no one thought to check. The only concrete evidence of Mr. Brown's visit had been an empty glass left on one of the suite's balcony tables.

* * *

Government Gulfstream 002 was waiting at O'Hare but its crew was expecting to transport a live Attorney General back to Dulles International rather than a dead one. The lead agent, who had overseen the transfer of the body from the ambulance

CHAPTER 23

to where it now lay - on the sofa of the jet inside a black bag - had been curt. "Heart attack," he'd said as he struggled to affix the bag to the seat so that the body wouldn't roll off should the captain have to make a steep turn. "An ambulance will meet you at the other end."

Gena, the attendant, had flown the Attorney General several times before and found him to be a man of few words. Now there wouldn't even be those. She'd prepared a jug of the lemonade he liked and this would go to waste unless she could find takers in the cockpit where she would much rather have been. Cooped up for one hour and forty minutes next to a corpse was unsettling. Whenever she looked at the bag she was sure she detected movement. Supposing the poor creature had recovered and needed air? All manner of crazy thoughts occurred to her. She was so disturbed by the time the body was carried off the plane at Dulles that she agreed to have a drink with the co-pilot whose interest she had been resisting.

Two days later a small headline in the paper caught her eye. "Attorney General Seymour Stone Dead," it read, followed by a short obituary. A cremation had already taken place in accordance with his wishes it said and a service of remembrance would be held the following week. Apart from a sister in Portland, no immediate family was reported. So that was it, she thought: a life over, just like that. But her focus was elsewhere. The young co-pilot had spent most of his two day layover laying over her and she needed him out. Her housemate had been visiting family in Idaho and was due back.

CHAPTER 23

CHAPTER 23

24

SINCE Attorney Stone's death the President had been
working harder than he had ever worked to get his initiative
through Congress. Favors were being cashed, promises were
being made and calls to act in the national interest were sounding
from the White House like the calls to prayer from a Moroccan
mosque. In the House, where Moralists just outnumbered
Nationalists and the majority Rationalists seemed to be leaning
his way, it looked promising. But in the Senate it was the other
way around and did not.

Henry didn't think he had ever liked Seymour Stone - the
man's inscrutable austerity just wasn't very likable - but he'd come
to rely on him. Power had to work in the shadows sometimes,

even in a democracy, and now his shadow-man had gone and died. The funeral, such as it was, had been a dismal affair. Only two other members of the government had attended out of duty, and had it not been for the honor guard the numbers would have been half what they were. Mary had excused herself. She'd never altered her view that his pick for the job had had 'a sinister look' about him.

The strangest moment, although in some ways a fitting one, was when the ex-Attorney's sister, the only member of his family present, had asked whose funeral it was. She'd come with her nurse, probably because her nurse wanted to see the capital and meet the President, and was suffering from dementia. Even those who might have wanted to jump on Seymour S. Stone's grave for an injury he had done them hadn't bothered. There had however been one generous bouquet of flowers besides his own, so someone else had appreciated him, but it bore no card.

As Henry watched the flag-draped coffin about to be lowered, he was forced to confront the sheer lunacy of human life. William Shakespeare's Macbeth had got it right: 'Life's but a walking shadow, a poor player that struts and frets his hour upon the stage and then is heard no more. It is a tale told by an idiot, full of sound and fury signifying nothing.' Henry had learned the lines at school. Perhaps his young self already knew where his old self was going.

"Eunice, will you try and get Senator Grasser for me."

The Senator was being as helpful as he could, short of burning his bridges to either of the other two sides, something a lifetime in politics had taught him it was rarely wise to do.

CHAPTER 24

"Mr. President, I have the Senator's secretary on the line. He would like to meet with you and could drop by around six."

Henry thought for a moment. He would have to miss the drinks party for Mary's brother who was visiting. He could forgive her for voting against him at the next election just to get him back.

"Tell the Senator that would be fine, and Eunice, could you make my apologies to Mrs. Dukes." There were situations his secretary could handle better than he.

Through the open door he would soon hear her negotiate with his wife. There were some appointments she was trying to juggle that evening, she would say, but she knew the President didn't want to let her down, etc., etc. It was a ritual the two played out. After some back and forth Mary would suggest the President skip his domestic commitment and Eunice, who Mary often said saw more of her husband than she did, would thank her warmly. He had been lucky with both women. They were the front and rear wheels of his increasingly rickety carriage.

* * *

"Arlen, I just can't get out of the goddamn hole I'm in right now," the President said. "Until this gridlock's broken things won't get better, whatever the Rationalists think. I'm almost at a point where I'm inclined to let the Nationalists have a shot at it."

"Stand aside for Meadows?" Senator Grasser said with a notable lack of enthusiasm.

The two old politicians sat on sofas in the Oval Office, bourbons in hand.

"Longbranch," the President said looking warmly at the gold liquid in his glass. "Kentucky's always been good to me."

"A pity they sold out to the I-Talians," grumbled the Senator, unhappy that ownership of one of his favorite bourbons had migrated to Europe.

"There are more Wops living in Brooklyn than in Ravenna, so it's not so bad!" joked Henry.

"I guess," conceded his drinking companion, reluctantly.

"I owe it to Mary, Arlen. If I do another four years there might not be much left of me."

"Since Missus Grasser died I've had no reason to stop. Besides Henry: I can't think of doing anything else. It's a drug, this politics. Once it claims you, the beast just won't let you go, and that's a fact."

"I think I could stop," pondered Henry, as he sometimes did when he was tired.

"Well let's not have you stopping right now my friend. This nation of ours needs Milo Meadows the Third like a dose of the clap - if you'll forgive my expression."

"That unscrupulous son-of-a-bitch is outmaneuvering me at every turn and I don't even know the half of what he's up

CHAPTER 24

to. Without Stone I'm flying blind. And you know the worst thing Arlen is that there are millions out there who should be supporting me. They just aren't playing our game anymore. They've given up."

"Which is a mighty poor reason for you to be doing the same, Henry."

"So what do you suggest Arlen. I'm out of ideas."

"Firstly, convene a meeting of the three faction leaders in the Senate; Yale, Studebaker and Meadows. They hate each other, but Yale for the Rationalists and Studebaker for the Mo-lists hate Meadows for the Nationalist even more."

"Why would they come?"

"They'll have to come: national interest and everything. Say you are searching for a way forward, with lots of publicity and then sit back and watch Meadows drive the other two mad with fury. That's the easy bit. The hard bit's giving the Rationalists an excuse to side with the Mo-lists."

"And how do you propose we do that?" Henry asked.

"I'm not sure. But I did point one of our young congressmen in the right direction and we just have to hope that he knows what to do with what I appraised him of, so to speak. We can't let the Nationalists use the dis-po-ssessed, Henry. The dis-po-ssessed have to come to you and the Mo-list cause. They have to vote and the rest of society must not be allowed to turn against them."

CHAPTER 24

"From what I am hearing, those people are not showing any signs of wanting to vote. And the Nationalists' bad-boy tactics, dressed up as coming out of their camps, are turning the 'in-work' against them. I even think some of our government agencies are coming to that position. We almost have two governments right now, Arlen and the power in my bit is leaching away. Calling me a 'lame duck' might be polite. A dead duck is what many are calling me."

"It was mighty unfortunate that we needed Meadows help us get Alpha-Omeega up and running. We can't brag about having all those scientists doing God's work. At least he can't brag about it either."

"It's too Old Testament for many Moralists: *A sword for the Lord and for Gideon*, as it says in Judges. But if we went around turning our cheek, our enemies would quickly devour us. The Israelis understand that."

"For sure, morality does not sit easily in the world, Henry. It just has to be fought for every hour of every day. What the New Testament told us was that fighting for fighting's sake is a cul-de-sac."

"I think it was back in 1960" the president said, "when the nuclear physicist Robert Oppenheimer claimed he had become Death 'the destroyer of worlds', that we allowed science to assume the role of God. Alpha-Omega was perhaps a poor choice of name for our scientific facility!"

"Perhaps we should have called it Bombast. I have always thought of scientists as being expensive plumbers and you don't expect plumbers to have any great metaphysical insights: although my plumber does not hold back from trying."

The two men talked into the evening about the lives they had led: about past campaigns and past successes – it did Henry good to be reminded that there had been some; and also about past failures which Arlen Grasser preferred to call his deferred successes. When the bottle was empty the Senator left and the President felt better.

* * *

The meeting did not go as planned. Janet Yale knew that with more seats the Rationalists held the advantage and could go either way. The problem she had was that they had to go one way or the other because their own program, which was essentially to let the economy heal itself, wasn't working – although as she kept emphasizing 'yet'. Doreen Studebaker quoted Keynes at her, to the effect that 'in the long run we are all dead' and reminded her of the great economist's put-down when a government official accused him of being inconsistent - 'when the facts change, I change my mind: what do you do?' But this only served to chill the air to near freezing.

In silent frustration, Henry watched as Senator Meadows went out of his way to be conciliatory to both of them. 'His worry,' he said, 'was the collapse in order taking place. The country was becoming ungovernable. Things just couldn't be allowed to continue.' He even managed to praise the President's Home Stabilization Initiative, which over the last two years he had worked to undermine at every turn, saying it was an excellent program but would take too long and did not address the immediate instability which, he claimed concerned him greatly.

His plan, he told them, was to empty the camps which he maintained were becoming sink-holes of vice, violence and disease, and to rehouse their occupants in underused military barracks around the country until a permanent solution was found. His soothing 'this might even be the President's own scheme' demanded all of Henry's self-control to ignore. Janet Yale seemed impressed. It was, after all a rational response to the situation and Doreen Studebaker couldn't deny that it might offer a short term solution.

The President reminded them that the situation had arisen because of a moral breakdown, and that while short term solutions were welcome, unless that was addressed they would be papering over the cracks. This angered Janet Yale who was still not prepared to admit that a system which had brought prosperity to millions was at fault even though, as Studebaker was quick to point out, it was now bringing misery to millions instead. Something was missing, the leader of the Moralists in the Senate asserted, and that something was morality which meant looking behind all the equations and paying attention to what was happening to real people.

As Henry observed the three leaders move inexorably toward no agreement because there was no agreement to be reached, he marveled at the sheer brazenness of Milo Meadows III. The man had a solution of sorts: sweep the human problem under the carpet and reenergize the nation around the idea of its own self worth in opposition to internal and external enemies. It was a seductive message whose appeal would grow along with

CHAPTER 24

people's fear, a fear the Nationalists were doing their utmost to foment.

Doreen Studebaker had fared worst in the meeting. The 'people', in Milo Meadows's terms, were those who had not been spat out by the system and did not want to be. Amongst them the Moralist message wasn't resonating. Even those who feared they might be next craved a quick, simple solution, not a complex moral one. In extremis, self-interest trumped interest in others every time. He consoled himself with the thought that Christianity had tamed the Roman state and that Protestantism had managed to establish itself against the implacable opposition of the Catholic Church. But these changes had taken centuries and he only had months. He needed a miracle.

He thanked the three leaders for coming and as they left, each observing the decorum of good manners so as to disguise what they felt, he thought that Senator Grasser might have been right in one respect. By the end of the encounter it was becoming clear that the Meadows charm had been wearing thin: like an over-rich flan, one can have too much of a good thing. Henry suspected both women would prefer to work together if they could find a reason for doing so. He just couldn't see one anywhere on the horizon.

Whatever meager uplift he might have gained from this insight was quickly dashed when Eunice came in to tell him that while the young student, Julia Somerset, hit twice when he and Mary had been leaving the Cervantes Convention Center, was expected to make a full recovery, Agent Roger Stimson had died.

"But Eunice, he only had a flesh wound."

CHAPTER 24

"Well that's what they are telling me."

"Please try to get the doctor who attended him on the line."

It was half an hour before the doctor could be located. Henry spoke to him at length. It was not unusual for someone who had experienced a severe trauma to suffer from a heart attack, he was told, especially if that person already had a weak heart, which according to his records, Roger Stimson did. The President asked if there would be a post-mortem and the doctor told him that the family hadn't wanted one and the hospital saw no need. So no, there wouldn't be.

First Stone and now Stimson: either he was becoming paranoid or the snakes were closing in.

CHAPTER 24

25

THERE was a sense of expectation in the air, a feeling that things were coming to a head, almost a mood of abandonment: all that could be done to influence the future had been done and now it would depend upon a throw of the dice at the hand of a god organized minds refused to countenance. Jay had left Washington, abuzz with rumors, but San Francisco was little better. The entire country, it seemed, was racing toward its rebirth because its old self was rotten and clearly dead. What would emerge from the brittle chrysalis no one knew save that it would be different.

When he received a text from Carrie saying that she was

flying in from Hawaii and planned to visit her parents at the ranch he suggested they meet at the airport and drive down together. Geraldine was in New York.

* * *

As they drove south they caught up with one another's lives. Jay told her how hard it had been finding his way around the corridors of power in the capital. She already knew about Alpha-Omega where John Franks had found sanctuary and the role Arlen Grasser had played. He hadn't told her about the 'Hospitality Centers' then but did now, mentioning that he had informed Mark Stetz at the Chronicle about them and was surprised the story hadn't broken. "That's awful," she'd said. "He's leaving it very late, surely?" And they agreed that he was, assuming his editor planned to make something of it. But what Jay knew about Herbert Hollingsworth he still kept to himself.

She told him that she would be working at the Haleakala Observatory on the island of Maui. He'd wondered whether being an astrophysicist was going to be a problem for her in the present climate. "Oh no!" she'd said. "The native people of Hawaii have an intimate relationship with the world around them. They even have a god for the moon. So me peering up at the stars seems quite normal to them. That's how they navigated, after all. It is all part of their religion which is protected by the *American Indian Religious Freedom Act* passed in 1978. You should know that Jay!" she'd joked.

It was after they left the highway and entered Gilroy that the sorry state of things imposed itself on their easy exchange. Every third store seemed to have been shuttered up. Small groups of Mexican Americans clustered here and there, waiting for nothing much. The one patrol car still on the city payroll wasn't even bothering to look for illegals anymore: most had returned south of the border anyway where poverty was normal and more easily handled. *For Sale* signs seemed to be spreading through what had once been the town's modest but neat suburbs like a virus.

They climbed the steep ridge behind the town wondering what they would find in the valley beyond. At first it looked much as it had always looked. Only as they dropped off the plateau and started down the gentle slope toward the Holden farmhouse did they begin to see the tents. Just small groups at first but when the flat grassland between the barns and the ranch house came into view, they found themselves staring at a tented city where horses and cattle once grazed.

"Did you know about this, Jay?" Carrie asked.

"Well my grandfather said he wanted to help out in some way, but I had no idea it was like this."

* * *

They found Madge Holden in the kitchen. She greeted Carrie in the detached manner her daughter ignored and Jay had grown used to.

"Your father's out patrolling with some of the men from the camp," she announced without letting go of the pot she had been cleaning when they walked in.

CHAPTER 25

"Patrolling?" Carrie repeated.

"There's been a group of hoodlums causing no end of trouble. They tried to burn the barn down a week ago."

"From the town?" Carrie wondered.

"No one thinks so."

"So what's their angle?" Carrie asked.

"Seems they want to make out the trouble's coming from the camp," she explained. "I guess they don't much approve of your grandfather giving these people sanctuary," she added, looking at Jay, making clear her evident displeasure that 'these people' had ended up on her doorstep.

"If they're from outside what business is it of theirs?" Carrie declared.

"Now why don't you kids take the old jeep and get some fresh air. Your father won't be back for a while."

Carrie had given up wondering why her mother made out that it was only her father she wished to see, but it was always the same: the vagaries of character. And as for them still being 'kids' in her mother's eyes – she quite liked that. It reminded her of simpler times.

"Jay, why don't you go on over to the ranch house and I'll pick you up in a little while," Carrie suggested. "If we hurry, we might get to the top end in time for the setting sun."

CHAPTER 25

* * *

With the seasoned growl of old age the jeep left the ranch house with Jay at the wheel and both of them now changed into their ranch clothes, which was just as well as dust swirled in and out over its windowless sides. It was strange seeing the presence of tents, of different sizes, shapes and colors where horses used to be, but they were well organized and didn't seem in any way threatening.

Besides, it was a big space and they were soon alone on the track winding their way up Castro's valley. The Mexican who had left his name behind in 1797, soldiering in the service of New Spain, could never have guessed what would happen to his land or to his name. But as Carrie had told Jay many times: when ordered arrangements became disordered the order that replaced them could only ever be understood in retrospect. She'd tried to explain why. It was something to do with the fluidity of things at the time of breakdown and the subsequent interlocking nature of order. The tiniest thing at the time of collapse could lead to order expressing itself in this way or that; to New Spain or to the United States of America and perhaps now to either a morally inclusive America or to a nationally exclusive one. She'd even said that there could be many different universes, each configured in a different way, but that idea had given him a headache and to his relief, she hadn't pursued it.

"Look!" she cried out. "It's the turkeys."

Sure enough, a hundred yards ahead, a group of twenty or so bustled across the road and up the bank like a coven of Franciscan nuns.

"That's a rather small group," Carrie noted. "Perhaps the rest have helped keep some of your grandfather's guests alive, just as the turkey once did our immigrant ancestors!"

"Oh I hope not!" protested Jay. "But you could be right. I'd have expected to see more deer by now too."

No sooner had he said it than they rounded a bend and came upon three black-tailed deer who stared at them curiously from a rise above the way ahead before scampering off without undue alarm. His grandfather did not allow hunting on the ranch but there had sometimes been poaching which he suspected was worse now.

They crossed the Pescadero Creek which was all but dry and began the ascent toward the redwoods and the ridge. The road was rough and pitted and would soon be worse when the winter rains came, gouging channels which Carrie's father would have to smooth out with the grader in the spring. The east-facing slope was already in shadow as the sun dropped ever lower toward the Pacific Ocean on the other side. They reached the crest and got out of the jeep just in time to watch what the Egyptians once called Ra sink large and red into a horizon far beyond the Monterey Bay to begin its journey through the underworld. Carrie's interest in the heavens was part of a tradition as old as human history.

He'd wanted her physically ever since receiving her text. He'd thought about it off and on as they had driven down from San Francisco and he'd thought about it some more as they had set out in the jeep. But now as sunlight faded on its way to starlight, the chill which accompanies that transition took hold and he

CHAPTER 25

found himself remembering the hot summer day when they had discovered each other for the first time in the grove near where they were now standing like two animals oblivious to everything save the intensity of a moment far more powerful than reason.

"Do you remember?" she asked.

"Yes," he replied.

And they led each other to the spot.

Like the vertical shafts of a cathedral the giant redwood trees stretched up around them, their tops just short of the stars which appeared as if a drape had been pulled back from across the vaulted sky embracing a universal sacrament as mysterious and absorbing as any the human mind had ever conceived. But it was unlike the first time with its innocent, overwhelming expectation. This time was assured with an almost ferocious desperation to blank out what they both knew but hadn't consciously admitted to themselves, let alone to each other: that this would be the last time they would know one another in this way.

As they lay there untangled side-by-side, uncertain and a little confused, they heard what sounded like Chinese firecrackers coming from far down the valley.

"Did you hear that?" Jay said, sitting bolt upright.

Carrie had but her "Yes" was hardly enthusiastic and she remained where she lay.

"Didn't your mother say your father was out chasing some

no-goods? We'd better get down."

* * *

When they made it back they found Bill Holden's truck in the yard and him inside the house covered in blood with two men from the camp standing by ineffectually while Madge, quickly joined by Carrie, attempted to deal with the injured man.

"Worse than it looks," one of the men said to Jay. "Just a flesh wound."

A flesh wound it might have been but even Jay could see that Carrie's father was losing a lot of blood.

"Has any one called an ambulance?" he asked.

"On the way," the man who introduced himself as Seb reported. "Harvey, Bill and I were patrolling along the south-east line when we came across them. They shot at us and we shot back. It was over in moments. They hightailed it and with Bill hit, we had to drive back. We're sure they are the same bunch that tried to burn down the barn and send a herd of cattle through the camp. We've asked in the town and they're not from around here."

"Any ideas?" Jay enquired.

Seb shrugged.

"Madge here says you're a congressman," he probed instead.

CHAPTER 25

Jay felt uncomfortable and imagined himself being escorted from the place at gunpoint.

"That's right," he admitted but was spared further elaboration by the arrival of the ambulance.

After the flow of blood had been staunched by the medics and a drip attached, Bill Holden was stretchered out.

Carrie said she'd be going to the hospital with her mother and that he was welcome to take the jeep round to the ranch house. He told her he'd be heading back to San Francisco in the morning. She told him she'd be staying for a few days, at least until she knew her father was going to be OK as it would be some time before she'd next be able to leave Hawaii. He assured her he'd look in on his way out. It was all rather perfunctory, overwhelmed as it was by events.

* * *

It must have been around half nine when Seb appeared at the ranch house door later that evening. In his hand he was carrying a newspaper bulletin which he thrust into Jay's hand.

"We want to know if this is true," he said.

Jay recognized the Chronicle logo immediately. It was a full page spread, with photographs, on the Hospitality Centers he'd learnt about during his trip to New Mexico with Senator Arlen Grasser. A reporter had clearly gained access to one of the facilities which looked more like a prison camp than the merry place its name implied. Under the headline *Forced Evacuation!*

CHAPTER 25

the article suggested that it would be Nationalist policy to round up all those in the itinerant camps that had sprung up around the country and parcel them out amongst these remote centers. The reporter had even included the copy of a Nationalist election flyer that thundered *Let's remove this rubbish from our communities!*

"So is it?" Seb asked when Jay had finished reading. "Is all that true?"

"I believe it is," Jay told him. "How did you come by this?"

"A van came by one day a few weeks back and the driver just left a stack of them. He said 'this is for you all and it's free.'"

Jay suspected this was the work of the Chronicle's editor Sherman Parish and the paper's owner Marjory Anhauser and wondered how far afield they had managed to go with it.

"We were wondering," began Seb hesitantly, "would you be willing to come and talk to us?"

"Certainly, but what about, specifically?"

"Well this, because not everyone believes the government could do such a thing and also whether there's any point in us engaging politically as it were."

"I'd be happy to," Jay told him without a moment's hesitation. It would be the first time he'd had an opportunity to speak directly to the dispossessed en masse which in itself illustrated the problem his country faced.

CHAPTER 25

* * *

Seb led him to an open area in the middle of the encampment. The arrangement seemed ancient: space for the private and familial next to space for collective action and experience. A fire burned and people started to draw in from the surrounding habitations. As soon as there were a good number Seb made a cursory introduction.

"We have a man from the government here and he's come to talk to us." That was it.

Jay looked at the faces around him, half lit by the flames, staring without expression or enthusiasm but willing to be distracted as they might be by the rerun of an old movie.

Not wishing either to preach or to harangue he began in a measured, conversational voice. "Seb here said you wanted to know two things: was what you read in the Chronicle broadsheet true and if it was, could the government do it? But before I answer those two questions, can I say that I am not from the government but rather am someone elected to hold the government to account.

"Now your questions. As to the first, do these so-called Hospitality Centers exist? My answer is yes they do. I have seen one in New Mexico and I believe it was me who prompted the Chronicle to investigate. As to your second question, could the government force everyone from camps like this into these centers? My answer again is yes. A President can do this by Executive Order, although practically he would need to have a majority in Congress favorable to the idea. At the moment

Nationalists are promoting such a move, although Moralists are against it preferring the President's Home Stabilization Initiative while the Rationalists in Congress remain undecided.

"It's gridlock and nothing's getting done. The longer this chaos continues the more those who are not in your situation will just want the mess to go away. This plays straight into the Nationalist game plan which entails sweeping the whole thing – that's you and people like you – under the carpet at the stroke of a pen.

"The President's plan is more nuanced. It is more complex, it will take longer and it gets to the heart of what went wrong in the first place. It will change the way society works and at the moment Rationalists, who are still holding to the view that the old way was based on sound scientific principles, are not ready to countenance that. But I believe they are leaning in the Nationalist direction."

Jay stopped talking and stared back at the faces staring at him and wondered if anything he had said made sense to people who had been abandoned by the world he was part of and were now building something separate to replace it.

"What are we supposed to do?"

The question came from somewhere in the crowd and he couldn't even identify who had asked it. But that didn't seem to matter because it was the question everyone wished to ask.

"If you don't vote for Moralist candidates, the Nationalists will win. That's really all I can say."

CHAPTER 25

Jay's answer was as simple and to the point as the question that had prompted it and for once had not been embellished by political hyperbole.

It was as the crowd started to loosen and as a murmur spread amongst it that a tiny piece of metal arrived like an unannounced meteor from outer space set on a course that would change everything and nothing. Jay Chandler fell to the ground at the same time as the distant rifle crack merged with the crackle of wood on the fire. Only those at the front noticed at first. One minute standing and the next limp on the ground like a deflated balloon. In the manner of curious cattle the crowd closed in around the collapsed congressman while Seb, on all fours, searched for signs of life. There were none. A gasp of primal anguish replaced the earlier warm hum of interest. It was as if a long lost friend had suddenly appeared from nowhere only to be as suddenly snatched away.

Within the hearts of some men present, horror mutated into anger and they chased off into the darkness to find the author of the act, but it was useless.

CHAPTER 25

26

"GET me Commanding General Crabb please Eunice," President Dukes all but shouted. "We need the goddamn National Guard to start doing its job."

"I am trying Mr. President, but I'm being told by his office that they can't locate him."

"Jesus, Eunice. What the hell's going on! That unit comes under the President's direct command, but this President can't do squat-diddly if he isn't able to get hold of his goddamn general!"

"Language Mr. President, please", Eunice prompted in a rare break from protocol.

"I'm sorry Eunice, but this is a goddamn disaster. We have what looks like a mob descending on the Capitol and I can't do one sorrowful thing about it! Put me through to the Commander's office."

Eunice realized she was fighting a losing battle and reluctantly accepted that in the circumstances her President should be granted a little slack. The situation outside was indeed grim.

"I have Sergeant Pepperdine from the Commander's office on the line now."

"Pepperdine, this is your President and in case no one told you, I am in charge of your unit. Now where the hell is your Commander?...."

"That simply isn't good enough, Pepperdine. You tell General Crabb that I want him here in my office in the White House in fifteen minutes. Have you got that?...."

"Well you do that son."

* * *

"This is your girl in the air, Sandy Vanocur, bringing you all the news that is the news from the NBC helicopter high above our nation's capital - And I have to tell you that the news today is forbidding, yes forbidding - Our seat of government is under attack - There is no other way to put it: under attack - Not by the British, not by the Russians and not even by the Chinese but by some of our own people – Our own people:

CHAPTER 26

incensed at their government's inability to pull the country out of the mess it is in - There are tens of thousands: yes you heard me right - I estimate many tens of thousands are marching up Southeast Pennsylvania Avenue toward the Capitol buildings."

* * *

"Mr. President, I have Senator Grasser on the line."

"Arlen....

"Yes, it's a goddamn disaster....

"Jesus, you think I don't know that....

"I've been trying to get Crabb all morning. His office says they can't locate him....

"Of course it's bullshit....

"Just a minute Arlen, I think that's his office now. I'll put you on hold."

"Yes Pepperdine. So what have you got for me?....

"The goddamn general's gone fishing? Are you trying to jerk my chain son?....

"Now listen, I couldn't give a damn if he had leave coming. You find what stream, lake or ocean he's on and have him call me - now. Who the hell is his second-in-command?...

CHAPTER 26

"Well you get Colonel Straker to call me....

"He's on leave too: you're kidding me?....

"Well Pepperdine, it looks as though it's just you and me. So here's what you're to do. I want the Guard deployed now - you issue my order: that's the President's order. You got that son?...

"Very well. You do that."

"Arlen, you won't believe this. The Commanding General's off fishing somewhere and his number two's on leave as well. Right now it's me and Staff Sergeant Pepperdine....

"Yes I bet Meadows is grinning from ear to ear."

* * *

"They have reached Seaward Square and are in sight of the Library of Congress - It's just a sea of people: a human tsunami - A trail of smoke is visible all the way back down Pennsylvania Avenue - This is one angry crowd - I wouldn't want to be in the Capitol Buildings right now - Wait, yes - We are now going live to my colleague on the ground Justin Henshaw - Justin, how's it looking?"

"Sandy, we're on the corner of Second and Independence Avenue - My cameraman will show our viewers what it is like facing an advancing army - As you can see, those at the front are carrying sticks - I've heard reports of shots being fired - It is slow-moving but relentless - The front runners dive into the buildings on the left and on the right to cause havoc - The cost of all this is going to be huge - Why hasn't the President deployed the National Guard? - That is what people are asking - That is what I am asking - Is there any sign of them from the air Sandy"

"Nothing that I can see Justin - The Capitol Buildings and the White House look completely exposed - I can see some police vehicles, but that's it - Are we witnessing the dying days of this administration? - We have a video link coming in from a member of the public - Where are you Sir?"

An unsteady video clip showing frightened customers watching men with sticks hammering at the other side of large plate glass windows appeared on the network's screens accompanied by a few anxious words "We're in the Oyster Bar on Pennsylvania Avenue. This is crazy. What the hell are these people doing? They are behaving like animals….." The clip and the words stop.

"You saw that Justin?"

"We certainly did Sandy - Vicious stuff."

"You might want to move, Justin - These people aren't taking prisoners."

"We'll hold on here for a while longer."

"Justin we are seeing crowds gathering on the far side of the Potomac - We're flying over to investigate - You take care now."

* * *

CHAPTER 26

The White House and Congress were being evacuated save for a core of the President's advisors assembled in the Oval Office, all staring impotently at television screens. In his Senate chambers Milo Meadows III was also looking at the incoming news reports. His plan was simple. When all appeared lost and the White House was under siege, he would descend as if from heaven like the Angel of the Lord to calm the situation and in due course be carried to power on the shoulders of a grateful nation.

Over the preceding months the Nationalist press had gone into hyperdrive. *How many murders before the President acts?* had thundered the National Bugle. *Are camps not hotbeds of vice and criminality?* had bellowed the Stars and Stripes. The Moralist-inclined media had struggled to land any knockout blows because reference to the gridlock in Congress and calls for action only lent weight to the Nationalist argument. An in-depth enquiry by the Chronicle's Mark Stetz into the death of Freja Olsen should have won a Pulitzer prize but instead was largely ignored. The two young men held responsible for her death were naive and stupid but their claim not to have acted alone had never been properly investigated in spite of evidence to support it.

Henry Dukes had slipped into the private quarters to urge Mary to leave along with Eunice, but neither lady was showing any intention of complying with this Presidential order, which Henry said was pretty much par for the course at the present time. He was on his way back to the Oval Office accompanied by the First Lady, who said she was bored sitting alone, when he was intercepted in the corridor by an excited aide.

"Mr. President, Mr. President, come quickly. You must see this!"

CHAPTER 26

Henry hurried as quickly as decorum permitted and entered the Oval Office to find his team fixated on the screens set up to give the head of state some idea what was going on in his domain. The favored network was NBC largely on account of Sandy Vanocur whose attractive manner was as popular with the women as the men, although perhaps with the former only on account of her safe distance. Able to make even the daily traffic report exciting, her commentary was rising to new heights of hyperbole.

"This is incredible, quite incredible - People are massing on the far side of the Arlington Memorial Bridge - Memorial Circle, Washington Boulevard and Arlington Boulevard are jammed tight with buses - Hundreds of them - You can see for yourselves - I've never seen anything like it - They are starting to cross - Row upon row - In tight formation - Disciplined - What a contrast to what is happening on Pennsylvania Avenue - Oh my heavens! - I'm seeing units of the National Guard assemble on the near side of the bridge around the Lincoln Memorial - They seem to be preparing to block the Arlington marchers - I'm being told we have a reporter on the ground, Angie Carmichael - Angie, what is going on?"

"Sandy, I'm here with the marchers on the Arlington bridge - The Reverend Dr. Richard Preston and his wife Abigail have organized this march - Reverend, why are you and all these people with you marching?"

"We are here to support the President," he answered, which evoked a cheer from inside the Oval office. "For too long, too many people's voices have not been heard. Today we aim to change that."

"Sandy, you heard it from Reverend Preston - But wait a minute - It looks as though we are not going to be allowed off the bridge - The National Guard has the far end blocked."

A groan came from the assembled group around the President.

Eunice rushed into her office to pick up the ringing phone while everyone else stood transfixed by the unfolding drama. The sounding intercom on the presidential desk was hardly noticed.

"Mr. President, I think you are wanted," an aide prompted.

"Thank you Jeff…. Yes Eunice, what is it?"

"You won't believe this, but I have General Crabb on the line!"

"Well I'll be! Put him through …. General, good fishing? …. Oh never mind. Now what the hell's going on?....

"You're deploying, as I instructed?....

"Jesus General, shouldn't you be defending the Capitol Buildings?....

"No, I mean from the Pennsylvania Avenue mob. They are the ones threatening…

"Now don't give me your professional judgment crap…

Those in the room were now torn between the President's

blue language and what was being reported.

"Well that's exactly what I intend to do General – you are relieved," and with that the President slammed down the telephone.

"Eunice, do I still have a driver?"

"I think Matthew's in the building."

"Good. Can you have him bring round the car?"

"What are you planning to do?" Mary asked, as everyone stopped staring at the broadcast and stared at their President instead.

"I am going to the Arlington Bridge and I'm going to join the Reverend Preston."

"Well then I'm coming too," Mary announced.

Henry Dukes looked at his wife for a moment and she looked right back.

"OK then," he said. "Let's go!"

Everyone in the room broke into spontaneous applause.

* * *

"This is Justin Henshaw reporting - My cameraman and I have retreated behind the Library of Congress which as you can see is being trashed - Flames are coming from the magnificent Thomas Jefferson building - This is an unfolding tragedy - We are pulling back to the Capitol Buildings - The mob is approaching our center of government - This is beginning to look like the storming of the Bastille save that our inmates are prisoners of their own delusions - The White House must be next - Where IS our National Guard? - What are you seeing Sandy?"

"Justin, a black limousine is approaching the Lincoln Memorial where Guard Units have been deployed to stop the marchers on the Arlington Bridge ....."

* * *

"You can't come here driver," a soldier barked at Matthew who had lowered his window and got as far as he could.

"Like hell I can't," snapped back the President getting out of the car. "Where's Crabb?"

"General Crabb, Sir?" asked the soldier, still not entirely sure who he was addressing.

At which point the General himself approached and unlike the soldier, immediately recognized his Commander in Chief.

"Mr. President, it's not safe here. I insist you return to the White House."

"You can insist as much as you like, Crabb, but from here on, I'm in charge. Open the bridge."

CHAPTER 26

"Sir, I'm sorry," burbled the soldier who now had the First Lady and Eunice to contend with, as well as Matthew who had no intention of sitting in the Presidential automobile, armor plated and bullet proof as it was, while history was being made.

"Now Crabb, if you value your military pension, which you should because after today you will no longer be in the army, take your troop, deploy at the Washington Monument and stop the mob from getting beyond The Mall. Is that clear General?"

* * *

"We're now going live to Angie Carmichael on the bridge - Angie, what can you tell us?...."

"Sandy it's confused here - The Guard units blocking our way seem to be disassembling - Three figures are coming through - Sandy, you won't believe this - It's the President and First Lady together with two people I can't identify - President Dukes and the Reverend Preston are greeting one another - We are moving forward again - The Guard units are withdrawing...."

* * *

As morning slid into afternoon two human armies slowly converged around the nation's symbols of government. Here and there smoke rose from buildings along Pennsylvania Avenue. The Library of Congress had received the mob's attention as had the House of Representatives. But so far, the Senatorial end of the Capitol Buildings had been spared as the unruly crowd moved directly into The National Mall and started making its way toward the Monument.

CHAPTER 26

Now unencumbered, the multitude in the west began to fill the spaces on either side of the Reflecting Pool under their past president's pensive gaze. As his country's 16th, Lincoln had faced down forces intent on tearing his nation apart and his totemic image had watched similar struggles since. The current President and First Lady led the way down one side while the Reverend Preston and Abigail did likewise down the other. To the south, across the basin, the memorial to America's third president proclaimed his people's right to life, liberty and the pursuit of happiness, the very rights the western protestors were anxious to reclaim. In contrast to their eastern opponents, the Arlington marchers were ordered and almost eerily quiet. Also striking was their sheer scale.

As the Mall filled it became clear from the news cameras in the air that the numbers from the east were far less than those gathering around the Monument from the west which were still being augmented by men and women coming across the Arlington Bridge. Even the Guard units sandwiched between the two groups were starting to look inconsequential in comparison.

Like most people in America, Pietro LaBoucher had been following the news with a keen interest. The way Attorney General Stone had been dealt with had served as a stark reminder of what life would be like if criminality became the sole preserve of the state. So he made a call. As a pragmatist, and with a soft spot for God inherited from his mother, he concluded that the Moralist cause was preferable. Besides, without God who would the devil have to play with?

* * *

CHAPTER 26

"I have never seen anything like it - Well not since Martin Luther King addressed 250,000 - Of course I was just a child then - But the numbers crossing the Arlington Bridge today must be at least as many - This is truly incredible - Justin, what's happening in the Mall?"

"Sandy, all I can tell you is that the march here is breaking up - Not because of the National Guard, I don't think, as welcome as it is - The shock troops at the front - A hundred or so, I would estimate The troublemakers - They seem to have given up - They are disappearing into the side streets - Just melting away - The people behind don't know what to do anymore - This is quite extraordinary! - Is it too soon to call this a great victory for the President and the Moralist cause?"

"No Justin - I think that is exactly what we are witnessing - And who would have thought it just a few hours ago?"

* * *

The door into Senator Milo Meadows's office burst open and Arlen Grasser strode in.

"Well Senator," Arlen boomed at his now ashen-faced colleague. "Would you care to join me and show solidarity with our great President?"

As at that moment Milo M Meadows III had expected to be marched out of the building under armed guard, he readily agreed.

CHAPTER 26

CHAPTER 26

27

OVER six years had passed since Henry Dukes had been reelected for a second term. His Home Stabilization Initiative had been passed during the tail end of his first by wide margins in both houses. But the recovery had been a slow grind. Where homes had been left vacant, getting their previous owners back into them had not been hard. But if a foreclosed home had been sold problems arose, especially if the banks had foreclosed on the same house twice, which had happened in some instances.

Reliquifying the banks and their customers had been the easy part: far harder had been getting the economy to function again. Congress had dusted off the 1944 GI Bill, passed to ease returning soldiers back into society, and offered a similar package of free education, free training and subsidized loans to those who had been thrown out of work. Perhaps the biggest change had been a renewed focus on community with churches of all denominations playing an important role.

No longer were decisions made on the basis of a narrow sectional, economic or scientific calculus, but on the basis of their implications for human life as a whole. The pursuit of happiness was no longer seen as a purely individual matter but as a collective concern, and liberty came again to be recognized as a shared experience, not just a personal one. Science was eased off its pedestal to be regarded as a means to moral ends not as an end in itself, as was its soulmate, the market economy. There were arguments about what was moral certainly, but that was recognized as healthy and an essential antidote to the emergence of a prescriptive moral priesthood.

The work of Alpha-Omega emerged out of the shadows and there was less willingness to turn a blind eye to activities deemed to be 'in the national interest' simply because someone in authority had so decided. John Franks and the other physicists who had been willing to accept the government's dollar started to drift back into universities professing a new humbleness. String Theory and quantum entanglement were recast to embrace the central role of God's underlying morality in determining outcomes. The academic mind demonstrated remarkable agility.

Various attempts were made to convert Milo Meadows's Hospitality Centers into something useful but these had largely failed and most were abandoned. Fortunately, as the Scottish economist Adam Smith once observed, a nation can absorb a lot of mistakes.

CHAPTER 27

Things had been done during the crisis, as things are always done during every crisis, which showed the human character in a very poor light. Secrets can rarely be hidden forever. But the desire to unearth the truth was not yet matched by a desire for retribution. For the time being at least, most people seemed prepared to follow Romans 12, 19-20 and leave vengeance to the Lord.

* * *

Carrie had married a fellow astrophysicist, Hamish Maclean. They had two children and lived in Kahului. Her parents were now retired having moved into a small house in Gilroy and had visited Maui numerous times. Old man Chandler had sold the ranch as soon as those in the camp had found their way back into proper homes. He'd have sold it sooner had it not been for them. The death of his grandson hit him hard.

* * *

The drive up to the Haleakala observatory, which Carrie sometimes did two or three times a week to check data, entailed negotiating over thirty hairpin bends and a traverse along the rim of the two volcanoes that had brought the island into existence. Often high above the clouds, its barren beauty had a special charm and made it easier for her to think about such esoteric things as why the implosion of a dying star became an explosion, or what determined the speed with which stars rotated around their galaxies. She often thought that it was as well she had married another astrophysicist. Their concerns were hardly run-of-the-mill.

* * *

CHAPTER 27

Carrie had come to Honolulu with her husband to receive an award from a new President, two years into her first term, anxious to rehabilitate science although not to return it to the pedestal from which some of its more voluble practitioners had assumed unwarranted moral superiority. Good citizens would be receiving awards alongside her.

The Governor's offices were ablaze with lights and full of flowers appropriate to the occasion. While Hamish sat in the audience she was ushered into line. Eventually her turn came and she was presented with a presidential medal. A few quick words were to be expected but the President's words to her were not.

"You knew Jay Chandler?" she said.

"Yes," Carrie answered with some surprise. "We grew up together."

"A terrible loss," the President said.

That was it. The line moved on. More awards were given. The following day President Geraldine Cooke flew back to the capital in Air Force One, dropping off her friend Marjory Anhauser in San Francisco on the way. Thinking about it all later Carrie called to mind the opening line in L P Hartley's novel, The Go-Between - *The past is a foreign country: they do things differently there.* Well it was and they had.

THE END

CHAPTER 27